THE DARK LADY

A Chief Inspector Woodend novel

The night after the mysterious appearance of the legendary Dark Lady on the road outside Westbury Park, a German efficiency expert, Gerhard Schultz, is found battered to death in the woods, and Chief Inspector Charlie Woodend is faced with his most puzzling case yet. Why did Schultz seem so frightened when one of his colleagues mentioned the legend of the Dark Lady?

"A very talented writer"
Booklist

THE DARK LADY

THE DARK LADY

THE DARK LADY

Sally Spencer

Severn House Large Print
London & New York

This first large print edition published in Great Britain 2001 by
SEVERN HOUSE LARGE PRINT BOOKS LTD of
9-15, High Street, Sutton, Surrey, SM1 1DF.
First world regular print edition published 2000 by
Severn House Publishers, London and New York.
This first large print edition published in the USA 2001 by
SEVERN HOUSE PUBLISERS INC., of
595 Madison Avenue, New York, NY 10022

British Library Cataloguing in Publication Data

Spencer, Sally
    The dark lady - Large print ed.
    1. Woodend, Chief Inspector (Fictitious character) - Fiction
    2. Police - England - Fiction
    3. Detective and mystery stories
    4. Large type books
    I. Title
    823.9'14 [F]

    ISBN 0-7278-7055-6

Printed and bound in Great Britain by
MPG Books Ltd, Bodmin, Cornwall.

This one is for Simon and Abigail, wishing them many years of happy married life together.

Acknowledgements

I owe a great debt to my websmaster, Luis de Avendano, who has not only created a superb site for me, but is tireless in updating it. And as always, this book would not have been possible without of the resources of The Brunner Library, Northwich, and its helpful staff.

Author's Note

The fictitious company in this book, British Chemical Industries, has its operations based in the same area as the actual company ICI. I should not like the two to be confused. Unlike BCI, ICI has taken a strong lead in environmental matters and – as I know from the experience of relatives and friends – has always treated its employees extremely well.

Prologue – November 1946

His shoulders hunched, the collar of his jacket turned up as far as it would go and his hands crammed tightly in his pockets, he made his way rapidly down the narrow cobbled street which led to the docks.

The fear, which had begun as the tiniest of grumblings in the pit of his stomach, had been gradually growing as he travelled up to Liverpool, until now it engulfed his whole body. It was not like the fear he had known during the war – a fear that with one slight error of judgement, he would be dead. No, this was much deeper. And more primeval. For the first time in his life, he was about to confront pure evil – and even the idea almost paralysed him.

He turned a corner, and lost what little protection the houses had given him from the chilling breeze which was blowing in from the sea. He shivered. He could have been at home, drinking a milk stout and listening to the BBC Home Service, he told himself bitterly. Instead he was walking towards a rendezvous he had not sought, and was now starting to dread. And why? Because, whatever his own wishes were in the matter, he seemed destined to become nothing more than the instrument of even-handed justice.

He reached the shelter on the sea front, and stepped inside. Half the windows had been broken, making it a far from perfect refuge, but it was still better than nothing. He moved into the corner and lit up a Woodbine. As the acrid smoke curled around his lungs, he turned and gazed towards the docks.

I shouldn't be here, he thought. I've already played my part, and this is none of my business.

Yet even as the words echoed around his head, he did not believe them. There were some things a man *had* to do, if he were ever going to be able to hold his head high again.

It had begun to rain slightly, or perhaps it was only drops of seawater which were spattering against his overcoat. He listened intently for the sounds of another human being, but there was only the lapping of the water and the distant rumble of the last

12

tram making its way clankingly back to the depot.

There was still time to walk away, part of his brain argued. It was not too late. Then he heard the footsteps, and knew that it *was* too late.

Looking through a broken window, he could see the man he had travelled so far to deal with making his way along the front. And there was no doubt that he was *the* man. The way he moved – cautiously and menacingly, like a wolf on the prowl – was enough to identify him, even in the darkness.

The man hiding in the shelter reached into his pocket and took out a sharp long-bladed knife. He made a stabbing motion, and wondered what it would feel like when, instead of cutting through the air, the knife sank deep into meat and muscle. It wouldn't be long before he knew the answer – just a few more minutes, and it would all be over.

None of the national newspapers had bothered to send a representative to the police briefing, and even the local rags were relying on their stringers, but for newly promoted Detective Sergeant Albert Armstrong this was a high point in his career. He was attending his first press conference, he would soon be investigating his first murder

– and he could hardly contain his enthusiasm.

He directed his gaze to the front of the room where his boss, Chief Inspector Harold Phillips, was just taking a cigarette out of the tin he always carried with him. Phillips lit the cigarette, inhaled deeply, rubbed the crown of his bald head with his free hand, then turned his attention to the reporters, who already had their notepads open in anticipation.

"I'll give you all the details we've managed to collect so far, lads," he said in a flat tone which suggested to Armstrong that this whole proceeding was boring him. "The murdered man was found in a shelter near the docks. He'd been stabbed to death. A single thrust to the heart." He jabbed into the air with his index finger, making even this gesture seem lethargic. "He was in his late twenties, had brown hair and was just over six feet tall. He had no distinguishing marks. His clothes were all of German manufacture, and it's our belief that he may have been a stowaway on a ship which recently docked from Bremerhaven. He had a set of identification papers on him, but on examination, these proved to be fakes." He flicked the ash off the end of his cigarette. "And that, gentlemen, is about as far it goes."

"What about fingerprints?" one of the reporters asked.

"We've had no luck there," Chief Inspector Phillips told him. "He's not on Scotland Yard's files, nor on those of the military or civil authorities in Germany. Still, that's hardly surprising – a lot of their records were destroyed in the last few months of the war."

"Any idea what the motive might be, Chief Inspector?" a second reporter asked.

Phillips shook his head. "No. As far as we can tell, he just stepped off the boat and got himself murdered. Could have been robbery – though he still had his watch and his wallet on him when the body was discovered. Could have been a random act of violence – the docks are a bit of a rough area, as I'm sure you realise yourselves." He rose to his feet. "That's really all there is for the moment, gentlemen. Thank you for coming."

"When will you be holding your next press conference?" said the reporter who had asked about motive.

"I've never been one to waste other people's time," the chief inspector replied, "so I won't be holding another one – at least, not unless there are any developments to report."

The Shipwrights' Arms was full of the usual lunchtime drinkers, but Sergeant Armstrong managed to find a table in the corner, and while his boss guarded the seats, he got the beer in.

"I'm thinking of taking a few days' leave," Phillips announced, when Armstrong had sat down.

"Leave, sir?" the sergeant repeated. "Now?"

"Why not now?"

"Well, there's the murder..."

"That particular investigation's not going to take much of our time. I'll send a couple of lads down to the docks to see if they can come up with any eyewitnesses – and we both already know they won't – but beyond that there's not a hell of a lot more investigating we can do."

Armstrong took a deep breath, and tried to infuse his boyish features with a manly seriousness. "With respect, sir, I think there's quite a lot that we could do."

The chief inspector looked at his sergeant through narrowed eyes. "Oh, is there now? And what more would *you* do if you were in my place, Sergeant Armstrong?"

Was this how the Old Man normally behaved, or was his air of defeatism peculiar to this case? Armstrong wondered. "Well, if we're looking for a lead, we could do worse than start with the man's identification papers," he suggested.

Phillips rubbed his shiny head again. "You're not thinking clearly, lad. His papers were fakes, so all they'll do is lead us up a blind alley."

"I don't think so, sir," Armstrong persisted. "It took an expert to establish they were false..."

"So?"

"So it must have taken an expert to produce them in the first place. Now, if we could find that forger, there's a more than fair chance he could tell us what the victim's real identity is. All we have to is to get on to the authorities in Germany and ask them to—"

"They've got enough on their plates, without having to bother their heads with this."

"Perhaps if I went myself..."

Phillips chuckled, but Armstrong didn't get the impression that there was any real amusement behind it.

"Fancy a free holiday on the continent, do you, Sergeant?" the chief inspector asked. "Well, you'd be much better waiting until a case comes up somewhere which hasn't had the hell bombed out of it. Not that the Krauts didn't deserve it, mind you. Did them good to get a taste of their own medicine."

17

It wasn't wise to get angry with a superior officer, Armstrong told himself – not even when he's just insulted you.

"It's not just the papers, sir," he said. "There are other things in Germany which might give us a lead."

"Such as?"

"His clothes, for a kick-off. Most of them were pretty shoddy stuff, but that jacket of his is quality, made by a real tailor. I don't know how many jackets that particular tailor will have made, but I'm willing to bet he kept a record of them somewhere and—"

Phillips's eyes hardened. "You've only been my bagman for a couple of days, and already you're off on a wild-goose chase, Armstrong."

The sergeant screwed up his courage even tighter. "I'm sorry if I'm speaking out of line, sir, but it doesn't seem to me as if you're very interested in solving this murder," he said.

Instead of exploding as Armstrong had expected him to, Phillips took another sip of his pint. "You never met my son, did you?"

"No, sir."

"He was a captain in the Cheshires. He took part in the D-Day landings and got through it without a scratch. Then they sent him into the Ardennes. He didn't come back from there."

18

"I'm sorry, sir. I didn't know," Armstrong said, but from the faraway look in his boss's eye, he doubted that Phillips had even heard him.

"His unit had a bunch of German troops pinned down," the chief inspector continued. "Reginald – that was my son – did the decent and honourable thing, and offered them the chance to surrender. They came out with their hands in the air, but one of them stayed behind in the woods, and when Reg stepped forward to take their surrender, the bastard shot him."

"I'm really sorry, sir," Armstrong repeated, and this time his words did get through.

"I'm sorry, as well," Phillips said. "More than sorry. That boy meant the world to me. So if one of our British lads has taken it into his head to stab some Kraut ex-soldier..."

"We don't know for sure he was an ex-soldier, sir."

"They were *all* soldiers. Bloody hell, they were so short of manpower by 1945 that they were drafting every available man – pensioners, and kids of thirteen and fourteen – into the army. So, as I was saying, if one of our local lads has taken it into his head to kill some bastard of a Kraut who didn't have any right to be in this country anyway, then I'm not about to bust a gut trying to find him." He paused, and looked

19

Armstrong straight in the eyes. "Have I made my position quite clear to you, Sergeant?"

"Yes, sir."

"Good." Phillips said. "The thing I admire most in the men who serve under me is loyalty, Albert. I reward loyalty. Ask any of the inspectors back at the station. But, if anyone ever decides to cross me..." He left the rest unsaid, knocked back the remains of his pint and stood up. "It's time I got back to the station. Even if what you're really doing is bugger all, it's always wise to *look* busy."

Armstrong watched his boss walk to the door. The chief inspector was a bitter and twisted man, he thought. And he was wrong in the decision he'd taken. Terribly, terribly wrong.

A crime had been committed, and it was the job of the police force to do all it could to bring the person responsible to justice. They had no chance of catching the murderer with Chief Inspector Phillips heading the investigation – that much had been made plain – but one day, Armstrong promised himself, the case would be solved, because he, personally, was determined never to let it die.

One

Chief Inspector Charlie Woodend looked down at the naked body on the slab. The dead man was in his early forties, he guessed. He'd probably been quite handsome, too, though it was hard to say for sure with half of his face stove in.

Woodend turned to his sergeant. "Give me whatever you've got so far, Bob," he said.

Bob Rutter consulted his notebook. "The victim's name was Gerhard Schultz."

"German, Austrian or Swiss?"

"German."

"It's sixteen years since I last saw a dead German," Woodend said. "Somewhere on the Rhine, it was. The difference is, he was a soldier, an' I was the one who'd killed him." He shook his head. "Thank God I'll never have to do anythin' like that again."

"At the time of his death, Schultz was employed as a time-and-motion manager by British Chemical Industries," Rutter continued. "He'd only recently been posted to this area."

"How recently's recently?"

"A few weeks before he was killed."

Woodend nodded. "Then the feller must have had a real talent for makin' enemies quickly," he said. "What do we know about Herr Schultz's movements on the night he died?"

"He was drinking in the Westbury Social Club until nearly closing time, then, according to several people who were there, he said he was going for a walk in the woods. That's where he was found the next morning. Cause of death – repeated blows from a flattish blunt instrument."

Woodend nodded again, and lit up a Capstan Full Strength to kill the taste of the formaldehyde which had invaded the back of his throat.

"An' what can *you* tell us about him, doc?" he asked the man in the surgical smock who was washing his hands in the corner sink.

"Not a great deal," the doctor admitted. "He was in pretty good shape for a man of his age."

"So he died healthy, then?"

"You could say that. He'd eaten a substantial meal about three hours before he died, and he'd been drinking."

Woodend inhaled, and was reminded how

adept formaldehyde was at wrapping itself around nicotine.

"So he'd been drinkin'?" he said. "How much? A lot?"

The doctor shrugged. "A fair amount. Given his weight and height, I would say that he was possibly tipsy, but definitely not drunk."

"That's probably the best way to be if you're goin' to get your head caved in," Woodend said.

Chief Superintendent Mather of the Mid-Cheshire constabulary – known because of his considerable bulk as 'Mountain' Mather – was not in a good mood, and when he was displeased everyone within range had to know the reason why. The person hearing him gripe at that moment was Inspector Tim Chatterton, a mild-mannered officer who was already working hard at acquiring his first ulcer.

"It's bloody typical of Sexton, is this," he ranted. "Calls himself a chief constable! Chief constable my arse. The station cat could make a better job of it than he does. An' as for backbone, he's got about as much of that as a worm. An' what's the result – as soon as somethin' a little out of the ordinary happens, he panics an' calls in Scotland Yard."

"A murder's more than a little out of the ordinary, sir," Chatterton pointed out in all fairness.

"An' now we've got a pair of London smartarses tramplin' all over our patch," Mather continued, ignoring his subordinate's comment completely. "Listen, Tim, you've worked with this Woodend chap before, haven't you?"

"Yes, sir."

"What's he like?"

Chatterton searched for the right words. "Unconventional," he said finally.

"An' just what's that supposed to bloody mean?"

How could he even to begin to describe Woodend's little ways? Chatterton wondered. "For a start, Mr Woodend's not got much use for police stations," he said. "The last case he worked on, up at Swann's Lake, he used the room where we'd found the victim as his centre of operations. He's not afraid to say what he thinks, either – and it doesn't matter who he's talking to. I believe that's got him into trouble a number of times."

Mather shook his head despairingly. "Do you know what the last thing we need on a case involvin' BCI is? The last thing we need is some sod runnin' round like a bull in a china shop. It's not even as if we *need* any

24

help. We've had the button right from the start of the investigation, an' now we've got the bloody coat – an' I mean *bloody* – as well. It's only a matter of time before we make an arrest, though I expect this Yard man will claim all the glory."

"I don't think you need worry on that score, sir," Chatterton said. "One thing you can definitely be sure of with Mr Woodend is that he always gives credit where credit's due."

"Well, I'm still pissed off that he's here," the chief superintendent said. "An' so – now it's too bloody late – is the bloody chief constable. But we're stuck with him, aren't we? At least until we can find an excuse to send him packin'. So I'm looking to you, Inspector Chatterton, to keep a very tight rein on the bugger indeed."

Keep a rein on Cloggin'-it Charlie Woodend? Chatterton thought. You might as well try bottling the west wind.

"I'll do my best, sir," he said, wondering how long it would be before he found himself on a diet of milk and raw eggs.

Chatterton's car arrived at the morgue just in time for him to see Woodend and Rutter coming out, and the inspector was forcibly struck – as he had been the first time he'd met them – by the difference between the two men. Woodend was nearly fifty, and had the build of a rugby player. He was wearing a hairy sports jacket, cavalry twill trousers and brown suede shoes with such a natural air that Chatterton was prepared to bet that the only suit he'd ever worn had been the one the army gave him when he was demobbed. Rutter, on the other hand, was dressed in a smart blue suit, as if he already was the superintendent he was undoubtedly destined to be. He looked young for his twenty-five years, and though he had a well-muscled body, he seemed almost dapper beside his boss.

Woodend stopped dead in his tracks, and let his mouth drop open in mock amazement.

"Well, if it isn't Tim Chatterton," he said. "Don't tell me you're goin' to be my liaison on this case?"

"That's right, sir."

"Well, that's a lucky break."

Despite himself, the inspector felt his chest swell slightly with pride. "Thank you, sir," he said.

"Aye," Woodend told him. "It'll make a pleasant change not to have to train yet another local flatfoot into seein' things my way. You do remember how I work, don't you, Tim?"

Chatterton sighed. "Yes, sir," he said,

opening the back door of the Wolsey for the two Yard men. "The first thing you'll want to do is – what do you call it? – 'clog it' round the scene of the crime."

Woodend grinned. "Very good, lad. That's exactly what I want to do." He climbed into the car. "An' what's the second thing I'll want?"

"You'll be wanting a pint. Preferably best bitter."

The chief inspector's grin broadened. "Accommodation?" he asked, as if it were a test.

"You'll be staying at the Westbury Social Club," Chatterton replied, sliding into the front passenger seat. "That's the place where Schultz himself was living, and also where he was drinking just before he went for his last walk. It's not really a hotel as such – though it does have guest rooms for visiting BCI staff – but the management is being very co-operative because they want this matter cleared up as much as we do. They've also put aside a room for you to use as an office."

"Well done, Tim," Woodend said. "You've done a grand job."

"Thank you, sir," Chatterton said, waiting for the comeback which usually accompanied any compliments which Woodend saw fit to bestow.

"Mind you, you *should* be gettin' good at it," the chief inspector said, right on cue. "After all, this is the third murder you've had on your patch in – what is it, Bob? Two years?"

"Two years," Rutter confirmed.

It seemed to Chatterton that this was too good an opening to miss. "Actually, sir, this case may turn out to be quite a lot less complicated than the other two you've been on."

"Oh aye," Woodend said, noncommittally. "Why's that?"

"While you were travelling up from London, a piece of vital evidence came into our hands."

"Vital evidence, eh? Tell me more."

"During our initial search of the area around the body, we found an old button," Chatterton explained. "Of course, a button's not much use on it's own, but this morning we found the coat it came off, thrown behind a hedge not half a mile from the crime." He paused for effect. "There were blood stains on it – stains which matched the dead man's blood group."

"You've shown me the hat, now pull the bloody rabbit out of it," Woodend said dryly.

"Several people have identified the coat. It belongs to a man called Fred Foley."

"Foley," Woodend mused. "That name

28

seems familiar." He turned to his sergeant for confirmation. "Bob?"

"He was a suspect in the Salton case, sir."

Yes, Woodend could picture him now – a short muscular man who wore a greasy flat cap and had dirty fingernails. "He lives in Harper Street, Salton, doesn't he?" he asked Chatterton.

"Not any more," the inspector replied. "He fell so far behind with his rent that eventually they chucked him out. For the last year or so he's been sleeping rough, but you could always find him if you wanted to. Now there's neither hide nor hair of him, but we've got men out looking, and we'll nab him in the end."

"So I'm about as much use as a spare prick at a weddin', am I, Inspector?" Woodend asked.

Chatterton reddened slightly. "I wouldn't put it like that, sir. Once we've arrested the man, you'll be invaluable in getting him to confess."

"Assumin' he did it. Or have we stopped botherin' with little details like that now?"

"Oh, he did it all right," Chatterton said confidently. "He was a commando in the war, you know, so he's no stranger to killing – and he's got a criminal record for violence."

"Threw a girl in the canal, didn't he?"

Woodend asked, as more details came back to him.

"That's right."

"Except that, if I remember rightly, he said it wasn't like that at all. He claimed the girl led him on, then said no, an' that he wasn't so much tryin' to push her in the water as just push her away."

"He did time for it," Chatterton pointed out.

"Oh aye," Woodend agreed. "Thing is, he wasn't in much of a state the last time I saw him, an' if he's slipped even further, then I can't really see him killin' anybody, even if he has had the trainin' to do it."

"We all think we've got our man, sir," Chatterton said.

"Well, maybe you're right an' I'm wrong," Woodend told him. "But until you've got him safely under lock an' key, it can't do any harm for me to dig about a bit, can it? If nothin' else, it'll stop my brain cells from goin' any softer than they've gone already."

They had left the town behind them, and were travelling down a straight, recently asphalted road.

"BCI built this for us for nothing," Inspector Chatterton said, as if he felt it was time to change the subject from Fred Foley. "They're very highly thought of around this neck of the woods."

30

"An' what did *they* get out of it?" Woodend asked.

"I beg your pardon, sir?"

"You don't get owt for nowt, as we used to say in Lancashire. What happened to the old road?"

"It's part of the area BCI wanted to flood."

Woodend nodded, as if he'd expected as much. "Why'd they want another lake?" he asked. "With all the subsidence you've had, I'd have thought you'd got more than enough stretches of water round here."

"Oh, it wasn't water they pumped into it," Chatterton explained. "It was chemical waste."

Woodend shook his head. "When are people goin' to start learnin' that they can't go around poisonin' their own planet?"

"It's only a temporary measure," Chatterton told him. "The experts say the birds and wildlife will be back in another thirty or forty years, as if nothing had happened."

"Well, there's somethin' for us all to look forward to," the chief inspector said sourly.

The road sign ahead said 'Salton', and though Woodend had been expecting to see it, he still felt his stomach turn over.

"This is the place where Mr Woodend solved his first case in Cheshire," Chatterton told the driver.

31

"It's the place where I nearly buggered everythin' up, an' almost got another little kiddie killed," Woodend said.

They had reached the village proper, and were passing between two rows of squat terraced houses with grey slate roofs. Woodend glanced down Harper Street, where Fred Foley had, until fairly recently, lived in complete misery and almost indescribable squalor.

Was it really possible Foley had killed the big German? Woodend asked himself. Even with the evidence pointing that way, he just couldn't see it himself.

At the other end of the village, just before they climbed the hump-backed bridge, was the George and Dragon – and inside, which was what was causing Woodend's stomach to churn, would be the landlady, the delectable Liz Poole. It had been a long time since he'd fancied a woman like he fancied her, and the feeling had been mutual. If he'd been the kind of man who could...

But he wasn't that kind of man. He had his wife Joan and his daughter Annie back in London, and that precluded any amorous adventures. Still, even with the best intentions in the world, he couldn't resist hoping that as they passed the pub, Liz would be outside, scrubbing the front step and presenting her fine rump to the world.

But she wasn't there – and as the car went over the bridge, the chief inspector was not sure whether he felt disappointed or relieved.

Woodend lit a Capstan Full Strength. "Is there any other way to get from Maltham to Westbury Park?" he asked the driver.

"Yes, sir. It's a bit longer but—"

"I don't care how long it is," Woodend interrupted. "Next time you drive me, that's the way we'll go."

They turned off the main road, and travelled down a country lane which was lined with mature horse-chestnut trees, looking their best in their summer green. Ahead of them was the entrance to the park – two gateposts made of dressed white stone from which elaborate iron gates must once have hung.

As they passed between the posts, Woodend got his first sight of Westbury Hall. It was an impressive building, with tall chimneys, gable windows in the roof, and a dome over the central balcony. Probably late eighteenth century, the chief inspector thought. It must have taken an army of servants to run it when it was inhabited by the landed gentry, and even with all the modern electrical appliances, it must still present a formidable task.

"So this is the social club, is it?" Woodend asked Chatterton.

"That's right, sir."

"An' who exactly is it a social club for?"

"It's for the people who live on the camp ... I mean, the people who live in the park."

Woodend could see what had caused Chatterton's slip. All the houses which made up Westbury Park were single-storied, long and thin, bringing back memories of countless army camps he'd been through in the war.

The car pulled up in front of the club, and Woodend got out and stretched his legs. He looked up at the almost cloudless sky, and at the swallows that were swirling on the air currents. He took in a deep breath of air, and suspected he would have relished it more if he didn't smoke so much – but even as the thought passed through his mind, he was reaching into the pocket of his hairy sports jacket for his packet of Capstan Full Strength.

Chatterton had got out of the car, and was standing next to him. "Shall we go and see where they found the body, sir?" he suggested,

"Aye, an' while we're gettin' there, you can tell me a little about the history of the place."

"The hall? Or the park?"

"Both of 'em."

"The hall belonged to the Sutton family from the late eighteenth century until the 1930s," Chatterton said, leading him between two rows of the brick dwellings. "Then BCI bought it."

"Seems to me like British Chemical Industries own pretty much everythin' around here," Woodend said.

"They're probably one of the biggest land-owners in the area," Chatterton admitted. "And they're definitely the town's biggest employer – there's not a family in Maltham which doesn't have at least one member working for BCI, and it's usually more. That's why the chief constable, Mr Blake, is particularly keen to get a result on this case."

Woodend sniffed. "Chief constables are always keen to get a result," he said. "An' they always want it yesterday."

He looked around him. The asphalted street was as quiet as one in an American frontier town which is waiting for Gary Cooper to stride down it, on his way to meet the men with black hats and a three-day growth of stubble. But just as in the films, the appearance was deceptive; as the three policemen made their way towards the wood, the chief inspector noticed that the curtains on several windows twitched.

It came as no surprise to Woodend that he was being watched. In fact, the surprise would have come only if he hadn't been. People needed the police to clean up their mess for them, but they wanted nothing to do with the inquiry themselves. That was why he liked working from pubs. Folk enjoyed going into their locals, and if the price of getting a couple of pints down them was a few minutes' conversation with a detective from London, then it was a price they were usually prepared to pay.

"When was the camp built?" Woodend asked Chatterton.

"Early in 1942. The Americans had entered the war by then, and the government needed somewhere to house all the GIs who were being sent over, so they requisitioned the hall and grounds – the hall for the officers to live in, the grounds to put up barracks."

"You know what they used to say about the Yanks, don't you?" Woodend asked. "That the only problem with them was that they were overpaid, oversexed an' over here."

Chatterton grinned. "Anyway, by the middle of 1944, most of the Yanks had been moved out," he continued, "and at the same time there was a need for somewhere to put all the Italians who'd been captured during the invasion of Italy, so Westbury Park became a prisoner-of-war camp. After the war ... well, you can see for yourself what happened, can't you, sir? There was a housing shortage, so BCI made the buildings a little more welcoming – putting a layer of bricks on each side of the wooden walls, for example – and moved some of their own workforce in."

"An' there's still a housin' shortage sixteen years after the war finished, so they're still here. It's a bloody disgrace," Woodend said, in the nearest he ever came to a growl.

"Oh, they're nice houses inside, sir," Chatterton protested. "They've got indoor bathrooms and all modern conveniences. Quite a lot of the people who live here really aren't looking forward to the day when their council houses are ready and they're moved out."

A small girl wearing an embroidered headscarf and a curious expression appeared briefly in the doorway of one of the houses, then slipped back inside. "Did you see that kid?" Woodend asked.

"Yes, sir."

"Didn't look very English to me."

"She probably isn't," Chatterton said. "You see, as well as the housing shortage, there was a labour shortage in this area just after the war, so British Chemicals recruited quite a lot of foreign workers. Polish refugees – that kid's dad was probably one of them – Italian and German ex-POWs who'd fallen for local girls or just didn't fancy going back to their own countries, and a mixture of other nationalities. So while the majority of the people who live in the park are English, there's a fair smattering who aren't."

"A veritable United Nations," Woodend said. "Wonderful! That should make my job a lot easier."

He was talking as if there were a real case to investigate, Chatterton thought – as if there weren't an obvious suspect already being sought – but he knew Woodend well enough not to remind him of the fact.

They had reached the edge of the park, and Chatterton pointed to a narrow track running between the trees.

"That's the way Mr Schultz went on his last walk," he said. "The path's about three quarters of a mile long. It leads right down to the lake. It's very popular with picnickers and courting couples."

"Why isn't it sealed off?" Woodend asked.

"It was for a time, but our boys have been over it with a fine-toothed comb, so there didn't seem much point in keeping it closed any longer."

"An' what did these boys of yours find

38

with this fine-toothed comb they were usin'?"

"Apart from the button from Fred Foley's coat, not much," Chatterton confessed. "It rained overnight, you see. Quite a fierce storm. So any tracks there might have been were pretty much washed away."

"Seems like the murderer had luck on his side," Woodend said. "Or maybe he had inside knowledge. Perhaps what we should be lookin' for is a weatherman with homicidal tendencies."

Chatterton was getting used to Woodend's sense of humour, and there were only a couple of seconds between the chief inspector's statement and the inspector's chuckle.

"I'm surprised you didn't find the murder weapon," Woodend mused. "In my experience, most killers who use a blunt instrument abandon it near the scene of the crime."

"I've got some men out searching the field where we found Fred Foley's overcoat," Chatterton said, and pretended not to notice when Woodend shook his head doubtfully.

They followed the path as it twisted and turned between the trees. "How did the dead man manage to see his way along here at night?" the chief inspector asked. "Did he have a torch with him?"

"We didn't find one if he did," Chatterton said. "But there was a full moon that night, so he wouldn't have had too much difficulty picking his way between the roots."

"You're sure of that?"

Chatterton nodded. "I tried it myself the following evening. It wasn't exactly as light as day, but I managed perfectly well."

"Glad to hear you've not just been sittin' on your hands, waitin' for me to arrive," Woodend said. "There's some forces I could mention that think just because they've called in the Yard..." He stopped speaking and came to a sudden halt. "We're gettin' close, aren't we?"

"How did you know that, sir?"

"I can sense it. I'm a bit psychic on occasion. It's nothin' to be proud of – I sometimes think all it means is that I'm slowly goin' round the twist – but there it is, an' I use it when I can."

"The body was found just round the next bend," Chatterton said, and when they'd turned the bend he pointed down to the root of a mature chestnut tree. "Just there."

Woodend closed his eyes tightly, and tried to conjure up a picture of what had happened on this spot a few nights earlier, but he appeared to have used up all his psychic powers for that day.

"Right, Inspector," he said, "where's that pint of best bitter you've been promisin' me?"

Two

The bar of the Westbury Social Club was an uneasy mixture of faded elegance and modern practicality, with a moulded ceiling gazing down disapprovingly on a formica-topped bar, and high, elegant windows serving as no more than a backdrop for stacks of empty beer crates. There was a billiard table, such as the one the original inhabitants of the house might have played on, and a dartboard, of which they would definitely have disapproved.

The only person in evidence in the bar when Woodend, Rutter and Chatterton arrived was the steward, a middle-aged man called Tony, with a bald spot on the crown of his head and watchful, interested eyes.

Inspector Chatterton ordered three pints. Woodend took a generous sip of his, then smacked his lips contentedly.

"It's a good pint is this, Tony," he told the bar steward.

"The secret's in the way you clean your pipes," the other man said complacently.

Rutter, watching the exchange, chalked another one up to his boss. By complimenting Tony on his beer, Woodend had won himself a friend for life – and a very useful one indeed. Yet to be fair to his boss, the sergeant thought, he would never have said the beer was good if it hadn't been, because in Woodend's eyes telling lies about ale amounted almost to sacrilege.

"Were you on duty yourself the night this German feller went an' got himself killed?" Woodend asked.

"I was," the bar steward replied.

"How many people were there in here at the same time he was, would you say?"

Tony looked around the room, and Woodend guessed he was counting imaginary heads.

"About twenty," the steward said finally.

"And you knew them all?"

"Oh yes, they're all regulars. This is a members-only club, you see – very strict, the management is about that – so we don't get any of what you might call passin' trade."

Woodend nodded. "When you get time, could you jot down the names of all the people you remember?"

"Sure," the barman agreed.

43

"Fred Foley was around as well, wasn't he?" Chatterton asked, ignoring Woodend's disapproving look.

"Yes, he was around," Tony readily agreed. "Drunk as a lord he was, much the same as usual. I don't know where he gets the money from for booze. He certainly doesn't seem to have it to spend on anythin' else. He can't have seen a bar of soap for months, his clothes are so worn they're almost fallin' off him, an' that dog of his always looks half starved."

"Oh, so Fred Foley's got a dog, has he?" Woodend said, suddenly sounding interested.

"He has. It's a bit of a mutt, but even though he doesn't feed it enough, I'd say he's quite fond of it."

"An' you haven't seen sight nor sound of this mutt since the night of the murder?"

"No."

Woodend turned to Chatterton. "Fred Foley's a hopeless drunk with no money an' very little initiative. In addition, he's saddled with a dog. An' you still haven't found him. Now why do you think that is?"

"Perhaps he's just been very lucky so far," Tim Chatterton said, unconvincingly.

"Perhaps he has," Woodend agreed. He took another sip of his beer. It seemed to be getting better with every mouthful. "Was

Schultz drinkin' alone?" he asked the bar steward.

Tony shook his head. "No. He was talkin' to Mr Hailsham from the main works."

"An' who's he when he's at home?"

"The personnel manager."

"Were they sittin' at one of the tables?"

"No, they were standin' at the bar. Mr Hailsham likes to do that. I expect he thinks it gives him the common touch."

Woodend made a mental note of the edge of dislike in the steward's voice, then said, "So if they were standin' at the bar, you'll have heard what they were talkin' about, won't you?"

"I ... er ... try not to listen to other people's private conversations," the steward said, warily.

Woodend smiled. "Come off it, lad. There's barmen who listen an' barmen who don't. You've got the look of a feller who regards eavesdroppin' as one of the perks of the job."

Tony looked sheepish. "Well, maybe I did hear a bit of what they were talkin' about – accidentally like."

"An' what were they sayin'?"

"Well, they started out by talkin' about jobs. Mr Schultz said he hadn't been here long enough to make any definite recommendations quite yet, but he'd already seen enough to be able to tell that somethin' would have to be done to make the company leaner."

"An' what do you think he meant by that?"

"Job losses, of course. He said that if he had his way, there'd be a fair number of people on this very park who'd soon find themselves lookin' for some other employment."

"Did anyone else hear this?"

"I can't say for sure, but I shouldn't be surprised if they did. Mr Schultz had had a few drinks, you see, an' he was talkin' rather loud. Anyway, after that Mr Hailsham started talkin' about the Dark Lady."

"The dark what?"

"The Dark Lady," Inspector Chatterton said. "It's a local legend. Nothing but a load of rubbish in my opinion."

"You may scoff, Mr Chatterton, but there's plenty of people round here as would disagree with you about it bein' rubbish," the barman said, slightly disapprovingly.

Chatterton smiled condescendingly. "Tell me, have you ever seen her yourself, Tony?" he asked.

"N ... no," the bar steward admitted reluctantly. "But I know a fair number of fellers who have."

"There's some men who'll see anything

and everything when they've got a few pints swilling around inside them," Chatterton countered.

"I'm gettin' a little lost here," Woodend said. "Who or what is this 'Dark Lady' exactly?"

"Her real name was Lady Caroline Sutton," the steward said. "She lived in this very house over a hundred years ago. Do you want to hear the whole story, Chief Inspector?"

"Aye, why not?" Woodend said. "I like to take in a bit of local colour once in a while."

"Lady Caroline was married to Sir Richard Sutton," Tony said, lowering his voice as if he were about to reveal the latest bit of scandal. "Well, he were a rum bugger, by all accounts. There wasn't a woman in the whole area that was safe when he was around – an' I'm talkin' about anybody, from high-class ladies to servin' wenches, with a few doctors' and clergymen's daughters thrown in for good measure. For years his wife knew nothin' about it, but finally she found out, like them as are bein' deceived usually do. As you can imagine, it came as a terrible shock to her, because she was still in love with him you see, an' as far as she'd known up to then, he was still in love with her. An' on top of that there was the humiliation of knowin' that all her

47

so-called friends were laughin' at her behind her back."

"Stop embroidering and get on to the bloody point, Tony," Chatterton said impatiently.

"If I'm tellin' the story, then I'll tell it proper," the bar steward said. "Now where was I?"

"She realised that all her so-called friends were secretly laughin' at her," Woodend prompted.

"That's right," Tony agreed. "She had been a very sociable sort of woman – well, your posh people were in them days, weren't they? – but she stopped receivin' visitors altogether. She'd stay locked in her bedroom all day, with the shutters down. But at night..." His voice assumed a thrilling quality. " ... at night, when everybody else was sound asleep, she'd get on her big black horse and ride around the country lanes for hours an' hours. Then one night the strain of bein' a laughin' stock must have got too much for her. When she got back from her ride, she went straight up to her husband's bedroom – they weren't sleepin' together by then, of course – and slit his throat from ear to ear while he slept. Then she went down to the stables an' hung herself from the main beam."

"And if you'll believe that, you'll believe

anything," Inspector Chatterton said mockingly.

"She still roams the lanes at night, her an' her big black horse," Tony continued, ignoring the interruption. "Not every night, of course – only when there's about to be a death in the district."

"People die all the time," Chatterton said. "It's got absolutely nothing to do with ghostly figures on horseback."

"An' the last time she appeared was the night before the German feller got himself killed," Tony said triumphantly.

"Well, there you are, sir," Chatterton said to Woodend. "Track down this ghost, and you'll have your murderer."

"She doesn't *cause* the deaths," Tony said sulkily. "She only ... what do you call it ... predicts them."

Woodend drained the rest of his pint. "I shall be wantin' to see this Hailsham feller from personnel as soon as possible," he told Chatterton. "Can you arrange that for me, Tim?"

"Yes, sir."

"An' while we're waitin' for him to turn up, what I think I'd like to do is go an' take a look at the room in which the late Herr Schultz had been livin' for the last few weeks."

Gerhard Schultz's bedroom was spacious and had a fine view over the part of the park which contained chestnut trees rather than huts. The dead man had been only in temporary residence, but he must have been comfortable enough, because in addition to the bed there was a desk, a sofa, a refrigerator, and a bookcase.

Woodend headed for the bookcase first, and Bob Rutter, who'd placed a private bet with himself that that was just what his boss would do, made no effort to hide his grin.

"Accordin' to young Chatteron, the room's already been gone over thoroughly by forensics," Woodend said, "so we've no need to pussyfoot around." He ran his eyes over the books. "A whole stack of stuff on management techniques – or to put it another way, how to squeeze the last drop of sweat out of your underpaid workforce," he grunted. "A few travel books – but all about travellin' in England. I wonder why that is. Ay up, what's this? *The Old Curiosity Shop*! An' *A Tale of Two Cities*!"

Rutter let out a loud stage groan. "Not another Dickens fan, for God's sake!" he said.

"There's more of us about than you'd think," Woodend told him. "He's got some other good stuff as well. George Eliot, Jane Austen. The Brontës. I'll say this much for him – whatever he was like as a manager, when it came to literature the feller had taste."

He pulled *The Old Curiosity Shop* out of the bookcase, examined it, frowned, replaced it, and repeated the process with another three books.

"Never been read," he said in disgust. "Now that really *is* a crime – havin' books like these an' never even dippin' into them."

"So why do you think he bought them?" Bob Rutter asked. "For show?"

"How do you mean?"

"To demonstrate how English he'd become."

"Either that or he was one of these fellers who are always meanin' to improve their minds but never quite get round to it," Woodend said. "Let's see what else we can find, shall we?"

The wardrobe was built into the wall. Woodend opened the door. Hanging at the left-hand side were several suits, all of them in dark colours, and all made of wool. Next to them were a dozen white shirts. Finally, at the right-hand end of the rail were three sports jackets and matching pairs of trousers. There were six pairs of lace-up shoes – one pair for golf – all placed so that they were exactly parallel to the sides of the wardrobe. In the tie rack were eight ties in muted shades.

"Impressions, Sergeant?" Woodend asked.

"The man doesn't appear to have been much of a snappy dresser, does he?" Rutter replied.

"No," Woodend agreed. "I'd say that, even for a senior manager, he was conservative. Anythin' else?"

"Very organised. Very military."

"Aye," Woodend said. "I bet he wore them suits of his in strict rotation. Let's see what we can find in the desk."

The desk had two drawers. In the top one were the standard elements of office stationery – paper clips, a hole puncher, a stapler, writing paper and several pencils. As with the shoes, they seemed not to have been put in there haphazardly, but to have been carefully arranged.

In the second drawer they found Gerhard Schultz's correspondence. There was a letter from a building society, which said that as soon as he'd found a house to his liking, he should apply for a loan, which the writer thought he would have no difficulty in obtaining. There were several invoices, marked 'paid', and a note from Schultz's bank manager in Hereford informing him that, as per his instructions, his account had now been transferred to the Maltham branch.

Woodend put the letters back in the drawer, and sighed. "What's missin'?" he asked his sergeant.

"Photographs, souvenirs, any kind of memento," Rutter said without hesitation.

"Exactly," Woodend agreed. "Remember when we searched Conroy's flat in the Swann's Lake case? We came out of that with a pretty fair picture of what he was like – or, at least, what he was tryin' to become. Here, we've got absolutely nothin'. It's almost as if this feller was doin' his level best to submerge his personality."

"Or maybe Germans are just like that," Rutter suggested.

"Aye," Woodend said sourly. "They've all got two heads, an' all. Here's a bit of advice for you, lad. You're a good bobbie already – you wouldn't still be workin' with me if you weren't – but if you're ever goin' to be a *great* bobbie, then you're goin' to have to stop lookin' for easy answers. Human bein's are a complicated lot of buggers, even the ones that look simple."

"Point taken, sir."

Woodend walked over to the bookcase, pulled out the copy of *The Old Curiosity Shop* again, and handed it to his sergeant. "Dip into this when you've got the chance, Bob," he said. "You can learn a lot about human nature from readin' Dickens."

Three

Woodend was halfway down his second pint when the door of the Westbury Social Club bar opened, and a man entered the room. The new arrival was in his early forties, had short black hair and sported a large handlebar moustache. He crossed the room to the bar with the brisk strides of someone who had taken his military training very seriously indeed.

"Group Captain Simon Hailsham at your service," he said, holding out his hand to Woodend.

"Charlie Woodend," the chief inspector replied. "Are you still in the airforce, Group Captain? I could have sworn that somebody or other told me you were the personnel manager at British Chemical Industries."

"So I am," Hailsham agreed. "Using the old title is a bit of a bad habit, I suppose, but it's a hard one to break."

"You've had sixteen years to try," Woodend said.

54

For a second or two, it looked as if Hailsham was searching for a good comeback line; then he seemed to abandon the idea and decide to change the subject instead.

"I expect the reason you wanted to speak to me so urgently is that I was probably one of the last people to see poor old Gerhard Schultz alive," he said.

"Aye, somethin' like that," Woodend replied, taking a generous sip from his glass.

Hailsham appeared to notice the drink for the first time, and shook his head disapprovingly.

"Strictly speaking, you shouldn't have been served that pint, you know," he said. "This is a members-only club." Then, perhaps realising how pompous he must have sounded, he laughed, far too loudly. "That's only my little joke, Chief Inspector. I don't suppose there's much chance of the law catching *you* breaking the rules, is there?"

"No, there isn't," Woodend agreed, declining the opportunity of joining in the merriment. "So what exactly can you tell me about the late Herr Schultz, Mr Hailsham?"

"What would you like to know?"

"Well, you could start with how long he's been in this country. If you know, that is."

"Oh, I know, all right," Hailsham said. He raised a finger in the bar steward's direction. "A gin and tonic, when you have a moment,

Anthony." Having ordered his drink, he turned his attention to Woodend. "Gerhard's been here – or perhaps I should say *had* been here – since 1941."

Woodend raised a quizzical eyebrow. "He arrived here in the middle of the war, did he? What was he? Some kind of refugee?"

Hailsham laughed again. "No, nothing of the sort. Far from it, in fact. He was a fighter pilot, like me. We both fought in the Battle of Britain – 'Their Finest Hour', and all that sort of rot. For all I know, I may have been the one who shot him down, not that he'd have borne me any ill will if I had. Comradeship of the skies, you see."

"What happened after he was shot down?"

"They put him in a POW camp, of course. Somewhere near the south coast, I believe. He was released in 1946. I should imagine his English was probably quite good by then, and he told me he'd developed quite a liking for these sceptred isles of ours, so he decided to stay on. Applied for a job in our Hereford factory. Got it." He winked. "He was probably helped by the fact that the personnel officer down there was another flyer."

"Cronyism of the skies," Woodend said, almost – but not quite – under his breath.

The remark flustered Hailsham, as it had been intended to. "Yes, well, anyway, he worked there until a few weeks ago, when he was transferred up here. He's been living in the club, but I know he was thinking of looking for a house."

"Family?" Woodend asked.

"I imagine he's still got some relations back in Germany."

"But not in Britain?"

"Certainly none that I know of. From what he said, I got the distinct impression he liked to play the field as far as things went with the fair sex. Would have been quite successful at it, I imagine. Good-looking chap with plenty of money in his pocket can't really go wrong when it comes to women, can he?"

The bar steward placed the gin and tonic on the bar with a little more force than was absolutely necessary, but Hailsham didn't seem to notice. He picked up the drink and took a sip.

"Yes, I wouldn't be at all surprised if he hadn't left quite a string of broken hearts behind him down in darkest Hereford," he continued.

"Well, that's certainly somethin' to be proud of," Woodend said dryly. "Schultz was brought up to Cheshire to be the company's new hatchet man, wasn't he?"

Hailsham gave him a sudden sharp look. "Who in heaven's name told you that?"

"As the German officers say in all those old war films, 'It is I who am asking the questions'," Woodend replied.

The personnel manager forced a grin to his face. "Gerhard was here to examine the viability of our operation and make recommendations as to how it could be improved," he said.

"To see who they could get away with sackin'," Woodend translated for his sergeant.

"We ... er ... do have a certain excess capacity," Hailsham said. "We took on a lot of new people in the boom just after the war, but there simply isn't as much demand now."

"Did Mr Schultz enjoy your story about the Dark Lady of Westbury?" Woodend asked.

"How do you know about that?" Hailsham said, shooting the bar steward a suspicious glance.

"I was talkin' to one of the customers who was standing near you that night," the chief inspector lied.

Hailsham looked a little mollified. "As a matter of fact, no, he didn't really enjoy it. I'd even go so far as to say that he seemed quite shocked when I first mentioned her."

"Would you care to be a bit more explicit, Mr Hailsham?" Woodend suggested.

"Well, I just said something like, 'What do you think of the Dark Lady?' and he went quite pale. It was quite disturbing, so I asked him if anything was the matter and he just shook his head – as if he were finding it hard to speak. But the strange thing is, the moment I started to explain the legend to him, he seemed to calm down again. And by the time I was halfway through the story, I'd say that he was completely back to normal."

"An' then he said he felt like takin' a walk?"

"That's right. He was from Bavaria, you see, and a lot of them are great walkers."

"So he didn't seem worried?"

"No, as I said, there was only really that moment when I first mentioned the Dark Lady when he seemed to lose his equilibrium. Just before he left, he even made a luncheon date with me for the next day."

"Did you leave at the same time he did?"

"No, I hung around for a while."

"How long is a while?'

"Couldn't have been more than five minutes."

"An' then what did you do."

"I drove back home to the bosom of my family, of course. The kids were both safely tucked in bed by that time, but my good lady was still up. She knows, from discussions we've had in the past, that I like her to

59

be waiting for me when I get home." He gave a sudden start, as if something had just occurred to him. "You surely don't suspect me, do you?"

"Here's another film cliché to add to your collection, sir," Woodend said. "I suspect no one – and I suspect everyone."

"But Gerhard and I were chums," Hailsham protested. "You could have knocked me over with the proverbial feather when they told me at the office that he'd been murdered."

"You'd have to say that, sir, even if you were as guilty as Judas bloody Iscariot," Woodend pointed out.

Behind his glass, Rutter was smiling. This, he thought, was vintage Woodend. Rattling the bars of the cage to see how the lion would react. Shaking the tree to see what fell out.

"I'll have you know that I'm a personal friend of the chief constable," Hailsham said.

"An' I once arrested a triple axe murderer who'd been to Rome an' kissed the Pope's ring," Woodend countered. "What's your point, Mr Hailsham?"

The personnel manager knocked back the rest of his drink. "I thought the police already had a suspect," he said.

"Somebody's been tellin' tales out of

school," Woodend tut-tutted. "Possibly your good friend the chief constable. Well, as a matter of fact, the local bobbies do seem to have a suspect, Mr Hailsham – but he's certainly not one that I'll be takin' seriously."

"In that case, if you're looking for someone else to investigate, you should start with the Poles."

"An' why would that be?"

"Because the Poles hate the Germans with a passion, and Gerhard Schultz was a German, you bloody fool!" Hailsham snapped.

He turned and strode angrily to the door.

"I thought you might just be ready for another pint," the bar steward said to the chief inspector, as Simon Hailsham slammed the club door furiously behind him.

"You must be a mind reader," Woodend said, reaching in his pocket for some change.

"This one's on the house," Tony told him. "I've been waitin' for years for somebody to talk to that prat like you just did."

Maria Rutter, who until less than a year earlier had been Maria Jiménez, twisted round in her armchair in an effort to get comfortable.

From upstairs, she could hear the sound of Ute, the Rutters' new German au pair, doing the vacuuming. The girl was very good at cleaning – very thorough – or at least, that was what Bob said. But there was no disputing that she was also incredibly noisy.

Maria tried to form a picture in her mind of what the girl looked like, but with only the sound of Ute's voice to guide her, it was an impossible task. If she could have run her hands over the au pair's face, as she would have done with a child's, then she would have some idea. But so far she'd been too embarrassed to ask Ute's permission to do so.

You've got to be more assertive, more like you used to be before all this happened, she told herself angrily. The way you act now, it's almost as if you're ashamed of being blind.

And why should she feel ashamed? Her blindness had come as the result of an injury she'd sustained from a police truncheon while protesting against General Franco's authoritarian regime outside the Spanish embassy. It was an affliction, but it was also a badge of honour.

There was the sound of footsteps coming down the stairs. "I haf finished ze cleaning, Mrs Rutter," said a heavily accented voice. "Vud it be all right if I vent out now?"

Did she have a fat face or a thin one? Was

she pretty or plain? Maria supposed she could always ask Bob, but there was that reticence again. As if she didn't want to put anyone – even her husband – to any trouble. As if she were hoping that if she said nothing, they would forget she couldn't see.

"Ute, would you mind if I touched..." Maria began.

"If you touched vot?" Ute asked, when it became plain that Maria wasn't going to finish the sentence.

No, she wasn't ready yet, Maria decided. She needed more time to prepare herself.

"I'm confused," she said, sounding it. "What I really meant to ask you was if, while you're out, it wouldn't be too much trouble to nip into a shop and buy a packet of tea."

"But I bought tea only yesterday."

"Of course you did," Maria agreed. "Where are you going? Anywhere exciting?"

"I am going to church, as I do most days," Ute said in her flat, emotionless voice.

What was the expression on her face at that moment? Were her eyes full of dreamy devotion at the thought of communing with her God? Or did she have the resigned look of someone who went to church only because that was what she had been conditioned to do?

"There's a ten-shilling note in my purse,"

Maria said. "Take it. Buy yourself something nice."

"Zat is not necessary."

"Please, I want you to have it."

"You are most kind."

As she listened to the au pair's footsteps retreat up the hallway, and heard the familiar sound of the front door opening, Maria shifted her position again. Her back was bothering her quite a lot, which was a nuisance, but bearable. What was really troubling her was the thought of how she would cope once the cause of that backache – the baby she was carrying inside her – was born.

Standing with his back to the bar, Woodend surveyed the group of twenty men he'd summoned to the club to be questioned about what had happened on the night that Gerhard Schultz had died.

Groups of men, he corrected himself, not *a* group. Because that was what they were – four distinct groups of men, each huddled protectively around their own table.

There had been a kind of artless choreography about the way these groups had formed. The first person to arrive – a large man with the sort of bushy moustache once favoured by Joe Stalin – had looked around him, then selected a table which, while not exactly at the very back of the room, was well away from where Woodend was standing.

"What's that bugger's name?" the chief inspector had asked Tony the bar steward.

"Luigi Bernadelli."

"An' what's his job?"

"He's a shift worker on the production line, like most of the other fellers who you'll be talkin' to."

The second man to enter the room had seemed to have no doubts as to where to sit. The table he had chosen was at the opposite end of the room to the one Bernadelli had selected.

"Heinz Schnieder," Tony had said, out of the corner of his mouth. "You know, like the baked beans."

And so it had gone on. The Germans, so it seemed to Woodend, had no objection whatsoever to sitting close to the English, but they made quite sure that they kept well away from the Italians. The Poles, on the other hand, didn't mind being near the Italians, as long as, in doing so, they managed to maintain a distance between themselves and the Germans.

"Is it always like this?" Woodend asked Tony.

"Pretty much," the bar steward said. "This place is a bit like four different clubs that

65

just happen to meet under the same roof. There's some mixin', I suppose, but not enough to write home about. On the whole, they prefer to stick to their own kind."

"Has there ever been any trouble?"

The steward shrugged. "Now an' again, when they've had a few drinks, there'll be an argument – usually about the war, of course – but it's never come to blows. Leastwise, it hasn't come to blows in here. They all like the subsidised beer they get in the club too much to do anythin' which might make me recommend to the committee that they should be barred."

"Right," Woodend said. "It's time to get this show on the road." He turned to face the BCI shift men. "Can I have your attention, please," he called out in a loud voice.

At the individual tables, muttered conversations gradually petered out. Woodend waited until he had total silence, then said, "I expect some of you are not happy about bein' here. That's perfectly understandable. But the plain fact is that you were the last people, apart from the murderer, to see Gerhard Schultz alive. Now, that doesn't make you automatic suspects, but you must appreciate that it doesn't rule any of you out, either."

He stopped to light a Capstan Full Strength. The killer could be one of these men, he thought – in fact, it was highly likely that that was the case.

"If the guilty party is in this room," he continued, "I'm tellin' him one thing right now – it might take me a while, but I'm goin' to find him. For the rest of you, I'm simply appealin' for your help. Anythin' you might have seen that was a little unusual, tell me about it. Anythin' you might have heard that could provide me with a pointer, let me know."

He paused to give his words time to sink in, and noticed that one of the Poles had leant across the table and was talking to one of his friends in a low voice.

The chief inspector nodded his head in the Pole's direction. "What's yon bugger's name?" he asked Tony.

"Zbigniew Rozpedek."

"Excuse me for interruptin', Mr Rozpedek," Woodend said, "but if you'd like to share your thoughts with us, sir, instead of just tellin' them to your mate, I'm sure we'll be very grateful."

Rozpedek looked up. He was around forty – as most of the men in the room were – and had a large nose and fiery eyes.

"I do not have thoughts to share," he said defiantly.

"You seemed to have enough a minute ago."

"I am merely translating what you said for my cousin."

So some of these sods didn't even speak English, Woodend thought. Things were just getting better and better.

"The way you can help is that *you* know what's usual around here an' what's not," Woodend continued to the men in general. "That's not an advantage I have as somebody comin' in from the outside. So what I'm goin' to do now is give you a couple of minutes to rack your brains for any little incident that evenin' which was out of the ordinary."

He could have asked them to think in silence, but he didn't. Instead, he studied the way they exchanged whispers. What all four tables had in common, he decided, was that each of them had a natural leader to whom the others turned for guidance.

On the Polish table that leader was Zbigniew Rozpedek, the man who may or may not have been translating Woodend's remarks for his cousin. The Italian table was under the control of the heavily moustached Luigi Bernadelli. A red-faced balding man, who Tony said was called Mike Partridge, ran the English table. And in charge of the Germans was a thin, intense man whose name was Kurt Müller.

Woodend let a full five minutes elapse

before saying, "All right, that should have been plenty of time for you all to remember. Is there anyone with somethin' he'd like to tell me?"

"It was a perfectly normal night," said Kurt Müller. "We stayed here until closing time, and then we all went home."

And by "we" he doesn't mean everybody in the room, Woodend thought. The only people he's speaking for are the Germans.

"We didn't notice anything either," said Mike Partridge, and Luigi Bernadelli and Zbigniew Rozpedek nodded their heads in agreement.

Woodend sighed. This was the response he'd been expecting, but it still came as a disappointment.

"You may remember somethin' later," he said, "an' if you do, don't be shy about comin' forward. In the meantime, as soon as my sergeant's taken down your names and addresses, you can go."

Rutter took his notepad out of his pocket, and pulled up a chair at the Polish table. Woodend lit up another Capstan Full Strength, and headed for the door. A walk around the park would clear his head, he decided – not that he'd got much in his head which needed clearing yet.

He stepped into the corridor and saw a woman standing by one of the tall windows.

From her stance, it was obvious that she was waiting for someone. And in all probability, Woodend thought, that someone was him.

He ran his eyes quickly up and down her. She was twenty-three or twenty-four and smartly dressed in a black and white check suit which played down her natural curves. Her hair was short, blonde, and tightly permed. She was wearing glasses with heavy frames, but Woodend would have put money on the lenses being nothing but plain glass. She was, he decided, a pretty girl who was doing her best to play down her prettiness.

The girl took a step towards him, and pulled a notepad out of her bag. "Chief Inspector Woodend?" she asked.

"That's right, lass."

She frowned, as if she didn't like being called a lass. "I'm Elizabeth Driver," she said crisply. "I represent the *Maltham Guardian*."

She put such stress on the words *"Maltham Guardian"* that she might have been announcing she worked for an important paper like the *Daily Mirror*. Woodend forced himself to suppress a grin.

"An' what can I do for you, Miss Driver?" he asked.

The girl licked the lead of her pencil. "Well, obviously, I'd like to know how your

70

inquiries are going."

"I've only just started my investigation, la ... Miss Driver," Woodend said. "Right now, if you've read your own paper, you probably know more about the murder than I do."

Elizabeth Driver smiled, but it was such an engineered, calculated smile that Woodend could almost hear the gears clicking it into place.

"You wouldn't by any chance be holding out on me, would you, Chief Inspector?"

Woodend shook his head. "It's always been my policy to co-operate with the press whenever possible."

"The thing is, covering this murder case is a really big opportunity for me," Elizabeth Driver told him – and the earnest, eager expression which came to her face suddenly made her look no more than about fifteen. "If I can get some of the national newspapers to take up my stories on the investigation, it could be my ticket out of the provinces."

"I wouldn't get my hopes up too high, lass," Woodend advised her. "This murder might be creatin' quite a stir round here, but it won't cause even a ripple in the nationals."

"That's where you're wrong," Elizabeth Driver told him. "It's going to create a huge splash."

"Trust me on this one," Woodend said. "I've investigated two other murders in Cheshire, an' neither of them has merited more than a small paragraph tucked away at the back of the papers."

Elizabeth Driver was smiling again, and this time her smile could only be described as triumphant.

"What you say may have been perfectly true for those other cases you've worked on," she told him, "but they were completely different. *They* didn't involve the Dark Lady, did they?"

Four

The sun had sunk behind the trees and, unseen by the two men who were strolling through the park, was casting its dying glow over the still waters of Westbury Mere. An outside observer – and there were several peeping from behind the curtained windows of the huts – would have said that the taller of the men was doing no more than stretching his legs and reflecting on United's chance of winning the Cup, whilst the shorter stuck to his heel like a devoted dog. But the outside observer would have been wrong about both of them.

From previous experience, Rutter knew that there were two situations in which Woodend's mind worked at its best. The first was when he had a pint in one hand and a Capstan Full Strength in the other. The second was when ambling, apparently aimlessly, through the area where whichever crime they were investigating had been committed. And on both sets of occasions, the best thing his loyal bagman could do was to take a back seat until Cloggin'-it Charlie's synapses had made their own – often unique – connections.

"What do you think of Simon Hailsham?" the chief inspector said, completely out of the blue.

"I find his whole attitude rather supercilious," Rutter replied.

"Supercilious," Woodend repeated. "That's one of them big words like 'rhinoceros', isn't it?" He laughed. "But I know just what you mean, lad. He's typical of your officer class. What's really got me bothered about him, though, isn't high-handedness – it's the conversation he an' Schultz had just before Schultz got topped."

"Why's that, sir?"

"Because, accordin' to Tony the bar steward – who doesn't seem to be a lad who misses much – the only things they talked about were the redundancies at the plant, an' the so-called Dark Lady."

"So what's wrong with that? They worked together, so it was natural they'd discuss BCI, and the Dark Lady had, supposedly, just made a rather dramatic appearance."

"True," Woodend agreed. "All very true. But from my experience, whenever you get two war veterans together the first thing

74

they do is start swappin' yarns, especially when there's some alcohol involved. Yet there you had a couple of fliers, both of whom had fought in the Battle of Britain, an' the subject never came up."

"The Germans did lose both the Battle of Britain and the whole war," Rutter pointed out. "Perhaps Hailsham was merely being tactful."

"Aye, tactful," Woodend said thoughtfully. "The thing is, tact doesn't strike me as bein' one of Simon Hailsham's main strengths." He stopped to light up a cigarette. "But let's put that aside for the moment – I think it's time we did a bit of visitin'."

Rutter took his notebook out of his pocket. "Who do you want to see?" he asked.

"One of the Poles. No, on second thoughts, I'll tell you what: let's start with the Italians. We'll have a word with that Bernadelli feller – you know, the one with a moustache like a scrubbin' brush."

Bob Rutter scanned his list. "This is Elm Avenue, and he lives at number thirty-two, so we must be very close to his house," he said.

"Then it seems like it was meant to be, doesn't it?"

They crossed the road and knocked on Bernadelli's door. A woman opened it.

75

Woodend's eyes clicked, registering the details: late thirties; hair greying, but still an attractive face; wearing a bright floral pinafore which was spotlessly clean and faultlessly ironed.

"Are you Mrs Bernadelli, madam?" Rutter asked.

"Yes, that's me," the woman replied.

She had what the sergeant had come to recognise, during the course of his other two investigations in the area, as a Cheshire accent – and there was a slight tremble in her voice.

"We'd like to have a few words with your husband, if he's at home," Woodend said.

She should have been expecting it, once she'd seen who the callers were, but the woman still managed to look shocked. "You haven't ... I mean you don't think he's the one who ... ?"

"We just want a talk," Woodend said gently. "Nobody's accusin' him of anythin'."

An expression of relief appeared on the woman's face. "You'd better come in, then," she said.

They walked down a narrow passageway, then turned left into the living room. Woodend's gaze swept the lightwood three-piece suite, the veneered teak table and the seventeen-inch television set. He noticed that the carpet, like Mrs Bernadelli's pinafore, had a floral motif, and that the brass ornaments on the sideboard had been recently polished.

"I must say, you've got the place lookin' very nice indeed, Mrs Bernadelli," he said.

The woman positively simpered. "Well, I do like to keep things 'just so' for my Lou," she said. "He works very hard, an' when he comes home he's entitled to a bit of comfort."

Rutter shook his head slightly, in silent admiration. A minute earlier this woman had been terrified of Woodend, and now he had her eating out of his hand. And as had been the case when he'd complimented Tony the bar steward on his beer, he'd managed to soft-soap the woman while, at the same time, being completely sincere.

"An' where's your husband now?" Woodend asked.

"He's on the lavatory," Mrs Bernadelli said. "We've got one inside, you know," she added proudly.

Woodend smiled. "It's a bit different from when we were growin' up, isn't it eh? I remember how I used to hate that journey to the bottom of the yard on a cold winter night."

"Me, too," the woman agreed. "Your candle was always blowin' out, wasn't it?"

"Course, the worst thing was when they used to come round an' empty the pans on a Thursday," Woodend continued. "The stink was terrible. I used to feel sorry for them sanitary engineers." He winked at her. "Not that sanitary engineers was what we called them."

The woman giggled. "We didn't used to call them that either."

"Still, we've put that behind us now, you an' me, haven't we, lass?" Woodend continued.

Making her identify with him, Rutter noted. Pulling down the barriers between policeman and potential suspect's wife.

"We've been lucky, Lou an' me," Mrs Bernadelli said. "You have to say, BCI's really looked after us. Lou's got a steady job, an' we've got this house. Yes, we've been *very* lucky."

But would they have stayed lucky if Gerhard Schultz had had his way? Woodend wondered. Or was Luigi Bernadelli one of those unfortunate workers with the German's black spot already against his name?

"I expect you have a lot of friends in the park, haven't you, Mrs Bernadelli?" he said.

"Oh yes, quite a number."

"Mostly English, would you say?"

"Well, yes, most of my friends *are* English."

78

"An' you probably see quite a lot of each other."

"A fair amount, I suppose. We all meet in the laundrette for a good natter, an' we sometimes go round to each other's houses for tea. Then there's the knittin' circle—"

"Don't you talk to any of the Germans or Poles in the laundrette?" Woodend asked innocently.

"Oh, they don't go on a Monday like we do," Mrs Bernadelli said. "The way it works is, it's the Germans on Tuesday, the Poles on Wednesday an' the Italians on Thursday."

"Is that a park rule?"

Mrs Bernadelli laughed. "Goodness me, no. It's just how things have worked out, that's all."

"And what about your husband's friends?"

"Well, let's see. He's got three really big mates. There's Mario and Giuseppe, then there's Leo an—"

The door from the corridor opened, and Luigi Bernadelli entered the room. If he was at all surprised to see the two detectives standing there, he certainly didn't let it show.

"Please take a seat," he said, in an accent which was a comical mixture of Italian and northern English. He turned to his wife. "Make us a cup of tea, will you, love."

79

He sat down himself, facing the Scotland Yard men. "I expect you are going to ask me if I have an alibi for the time at which Gerhard Schultz was murdered," he said.

"Well, that's as good a point as any to start from," the chief inspector agreed.

"Schultz left the club just before closing time," Bernadelli said, "so naturally it was not long before the rest of us left too. I walked part of the way back with some of the other men—"

"Mario, Giuseppe and Leo?" Woodend guessed.

Bernadelli's eyes narrowed. "That's right."

"Your wife was tellin' us about them. But I'm sorry, I interrupted you. Carry on with what you were sayin'."

"Mario lives closest to the club, so he left us first. Leo was next, and Giuseppe and me parted company at the corner. I must have got home at about twenty past eleven."

"Can your wife confirm that?"

Bernadelli shook his head. "She wasn't here."

"Why was that?"

"She was staying with her mother. The old lady had gone down with the flu. So no, to answer your question, I do not have an alibi. But I had no reason in the world to kill the German."

"The German," Woodend mused. "Now

that's what I call a very interestin' label to give the man. Not 'Mr Schultz', or even 'that bastard of a manager', but *the German*."

"What's your point?" Bernadelli asked.

"I couldn't help noticin', back in the club, that the Italians and the Germans don't mix," Woodend said.

"That's quite true," Bernadelli admitted. "But it is more of their choosing than it is of ours."

"Is that because they feel that your lot let their lot down in the war?"

"Let them down?"

"You know what I mean. They probably think that you surrendered to the Allies too easily."

Bernadelli smiled. "Yes, I do know what you mean. I know all the old jokes as well," he said. "Have you heard this one? How many gears does an Italian tank have?"

"I don't know."

"Five – one to go forward and four for reverse." He laughed defensively. "Perhaps you are right when you say that the Germans do not think we were very good soldiers to have on their side. But it was once we were taken prisoner that the real resentment started."

"Why should that be?"

"Because we were treated very differently.

We Italians were put to work on the farms. It was no hardship for me. You have to understand, I was a slum boy from Naples. I had never even *seen* a farm before." Bernadelli smiled again. "I thought it was wonderful to be allowed to work on such a place. That was when I learned to love horses. I still work in a stable in my free time. Not because of the money, but so I can be close to those beautiful animals."

"You were tellin' us about how you were treated differently from the Germans," Woodend pointed out.

"That's right. As I said, we worked on the farms. And we were paid for it – five shillings a week. It wasn't a great deal of money, even back then, but it allowed us to buy the little luxuries which made our lives bearable. I saved up enough money to buy a second-hand bicycle. And at the weekends, we were allowed to go into the town. We were not permitted to use public transport or enter any of the pubs, but other than that there were no restrictions on us. Many of us made friends with the local people, even before the war was over. I met my wife just after the Allied Forces crossed the Rhine."

"You were better off than me!" Woodend said.

Bernadelli smiled again. "We were better off than most men in Europe at the time," he said. "But life as a POW was not the same for the Germans. People around here remembered the times when their planes went over every night, on their way to bomb Manchester and Liverpool. They remembered all those hours spent huddled in shelters, where they prayed that one of those planes wouldn't decide to drop its bombs on top of them. As far as they were concerned, we Italians were just likeable clowns, and the real enemy was the Germans."

"So they didn't get the same freedoms you did?"

"They were wired off in their own special section of the camp. When we went out in the morning to work in the fields, we could see them standing close to the fence and watching us. And we could feel their hatred, even from a distance. Now that the war is over, they have managed to forgive the British – but they have never forgiven us."

"Gerhard Schultz was a prisoner of war, wasn't he?" Woodend said reflectively.

"That is what I've been told. But he certainly wasn't a prisoner here," Bernadelli said.

"No, but he was a prisoner nonetheless. An' possibly he had exactly the same experience of Italians as the Germans incarcerated here did."

"Possibly," Bernadelli agreed cautiously.

"An' now, finally, he was in a position to pay you back, wasn't he?" Woodend said.

"I don't know what you're talking about."

"Come on, Mr Bernadelli, you're far too intelligent a man not to have followed my line of logic. You did hear him tell Mr Hailsham that there were goin' to be job losses, didn't you?"

"Yes," the Italian admitted. "I did."

"An' where would those cuts fall? Why, as far as Schultz was concerned, they should probably fall on the Italians, who had had such an easy time of it durin' the war. Perhaps one of your lot figured that if it was someone other than Schultz who made the decision – someone who hadn't got anythin' against Italians – you wouldn't come off quite so badly."

"You're saying that he could have been killed to protect jobs?" Bernadelli asked, giving a fair impression of incredulity.

"An' homes," Woodend said. "You've got a nice house here. Lose your job an' you'd lose that as well."

The Italian nodded thoughtfully. "Do I need to ask to see my lawyer?" he asked.

"No, Mr Bernadelli. I'd have to have a lot more on you than no alibi before you'd need that."

Woodend and Rutter stood watching a

colony of bats glide around in the gathering twilight.

"A nice woman, that Mrs Bernadelli," Woodend said. "Makes a good northern cup of tea, an' has plenty to say for herself once you've got her to open up a little."

Rutter smiled. The conversation over tea had been about the old days and the similar experiences they'd had. Coming from a comfortable suburban home as he did, it had all seemed as alien as if he'd been overhearing a conversation between a couple of Eskimos.

"What did you make of the husband?" Rutter asked.

"I think he's hidin' somethin'," Woodend replied. "But let's face it, which of us hasn't got somethin' to hide?"

"And what do you think his secret might be?"

"Ee, lad, I haven't got a clue." Woodend checked his watch. "There's just time to make one more visit before we call it a day an' have the last couple of pints of the evenin'."

"And who will it be this time?"

"The Pole," Woodend said. "The one who fancies himself as a bit of a translator."

Zbigniew Rozpedek did not look pleased to see Woodend and Rutter, but after the man's hostile attitude during the meeting in the bar, the chief inspector had hardly expected to be welcomed with open arms.

The Pole led them into his living room, which was not as cosy as the one they'd just left, but was pleasant enough in its own way.

"I am having a vodka," Rozpedek said, walking over to his veneered teak cocktail cabinet which played a tinny tune when he opened it. "You may have one too, if you wish."

Don't offer us one, make us ask for it, the chief inspector thought. A very nice touch. But I've always been able to give back as good as I get.

"Personally, I never touch anythin' that's Russian as a matter of principle," he said aloud.

Rozpedek's eyes blazed with indignation. "This is *Polish* vodka," he said, as he poured out three glasses from a bottle with no label on it. He walked over to the two policemen and handed them a glass each. "Try it."

Woodend took a sip. It was perhaps a second before the incendiary device was set off in his stomach and someone hit him very hard over the back of the head with a hammer.

Rozpedek gave him a superior smile, and knocked back his own glass in one gulp. As he sat down, it was clear that he considered he had won a victory of some sort.

Woodend wondered whether lighting a cigarette would turn him into a fire-eater, and decided to err on the side of caution.

"What did you do after you left the club on the night of Gerhard Schultz's death?" he asked.

"None of us were feeling tired, so we came back here to play cards and drink vodka," Rozpedek said.

"The 'we' in this case would be ... ?"

"Me and the three friends I was drinking with."

"All of them Poles?"

"Yes."

"Your wife didn't mind."

"It is not her place to mind," Rozpedek said. "I am the man of the house. Besides, she had already gone to bed," he admitted, "and once she is asleep, there is no waking her until morning."

"Did you fight in the war?"

"Yes."

"An' where was it exactly you served?"

"I was with the Free Poles who made up part of the force which occupied the bridge at Arnhem."

"That must have been hairy," Woodend said.

"Hairy?" Rozpedek repeated, mystified.

"Difficult. Dangerous," Woodend elucidated.

The Pole nodded. "Later, they called it 'a bridge too far'. We were completely cut off from the rest of the Allied Army by the Germans. I lost a lot of my comrades that day."

"Who do you blame?"

"I don't understand."

"Who do you blame for the deaths of your comrades? The Allied High Command for makin' a cock-up of organisin' the whole thing – or the Germans who actually pulled the triggers?"

Rozpedek shrugged. "I blame no one. Mistakes were made, but mistakes always happen in war."

Noticing that Rutter's glass was still as full as when it had been handed to him, Woodend took a second sip of his vodka. It did not have quite so devastating an effect this time.

"How do you feel about the Germans now that the war's over?" he asked.

Another shrug. "They are just people, like we are."

He was being about as genuine as a nine-bob note, Woodend thought. It was time to start stirring things up.

"I remember the day the Germans invaded Poland," he said. "We all expected

88

the Polish Army to put up some strong resistance – to buy us time to get organised ourselves – but they turned out to be a completely bloody useless shower, didn't they? How long did it take the Germans to conquer the country? Ten days? It was a real walkover for them, wasn't it?"

The anger flashed in Rozpedek's eyes again. "We had cavalry, and they had tanks," he said. "Our soldiers fought incredibly bravely, but they were doomed from the start."

"And, of course, the Krauts had control of the skies," Woodend pointed out. "They'd never have done so well without that."

"That is true," Rozpedek agreed hotly. "Our army were sitting targets for the Boche fliers."

"Has it ever occurred to you that one of the pilots who took such unfair advantage of the Polish Army's weakness might have been a young flight lieutenant called Gerhard Schultz?"

"No," Rozpedek said – and Woodend could tell he was lying.

"The Germans weren't exactly what you might call benevolent conquerors, were they?"

"They thought of the Poles in the same way they thought of the gypsies," Rozpedek told him, his voice so loud now that he was almost shouting. "In their eyes, we were less than human. They closed down all the universities – even the medical schools – because you do not bother to educate animals. They sent thousands of us to the concentration camps. Their last act, when they retreated from Warsaw, was to blow up the old town."

"And you still hate them for it, even now, don't you?" the chief inspector asked quietly.

"Yes, I hate them!" the Pole screamed. "With every ounce of my being, I hate them."

Could it really be this easy? Woodend wondered. Would it only take a little more pressure to make Rozpedek crack and confess to the bloody murder of Gerhard Schultz?

"It was bad enough havin' to work with the Germans as fellow shift workers an' drink in the same bar as them," he said. "But then Gerhard Schultz arrived. A man who played more than his part in killin' your countrymen and enslavin' your country. A man who now had power over you. You didn't risk your life in Arnhem to be ordered about by a Kraut. Your comrades had given their lives to make sure such a thing could never happen again."

"I should have killed him," Rozpedek said.

"It's what any true patriot would have done. But to my eternal shame, I left the extermination of that vermin to someone else."

"One of the other Poles?" Woodend asked.

Rozpedek looked thunderstruck. "Are you asking me if I knew he was going to be killed?" he demanded.

"More or less," Woodend agreed.

Rozpedek shook his head vigorously. "I swear to you that I had no idea he would be murdered."

"An' what about any idea you might have had *since* the murder?" Woodend pressed on. "Has any of your friends said anythin' to make you think that they could have been involved?"

"No," Rozpedek said. "But even if they had done, I would not tell you." He stood up, walked over to the drinks cabinet, and poured himself another shot of vodka. "I do not know who killed Gerhard Schultz, but whoever he is—" he raised the glass and knocked back the vodka – "I salute him."

Five

Woodend stood in the doorway of Westbury Social Club bar and looked around him. The German and English tables were fully occupied – Karl Müller presiding over the former, and the red-faced Mike Partridge in charge of the other. There was only one person at the Polish table, a thin-faced young man who must have missed the war by a good ten years.

"I'm goin' to have a quick word with that Polish lad sittin' all on his lonesome over there," the chief inspector told his sergeant. "An' while I'm havin' my chat, you could do a lot worse with your time than get the ale in."

As he crossed the room, he was aware of several sets of hostile eyes following him.

Aye, well, I've never been much of a one for enterin' popularity contests, he thought.

He reached the Polish table and, un-invited, sat down. "I'm Chief Inspector

Woodend from Scotland Yard, as you probably remember from earlier," he said to the young Pole. "Now if the answer to this question is no, you probably won't understand a blind word I'm sayin' in the first place, but are you one of the ones who don't speak any English?"

"I am Mariusz Wasak," the Pole replied. "My parents left Poland when I was baby, and I have been in England for most of my life, so the language is no problem to me."

"But despite the fact that you don't remember your homeland, you're still a Pole at heart, aren't you?" Woodend guessed.

"I am a Pole to the very bottom of my soul," the young man replied with a sudden intensity, "and one day, when the communists have finally fallen, I will return to my homeland."

"If I was you, I wouldn't hold my breath while I was waitin' for that to happen," Woodend advised him. "Can I just get one thing clear? You were one of the ones who went back to Zbigniew Rozpedek's house on the night of the murder, weren't you?"

Wasak raised a surprised eyebrow. "You pronounce his name better than most Englishmen seem to manage," he said.

"I always try to pronounce people's names correctly," Woodend told him. "It's the least they've got a right to expect. Now would

93

you mind answerin' the question please, Mr Wasak?"

The young Pole nodded. "Yes, after the bar closed, I went back to Zbigniew's house."

"An' what did you do when you got there?"

"Why do you need to ask me? Surely Zbigniew must have told you that himself."

Woodend whistled softly. "I've just left his house, but you already know about it," he said.

The Pole gave him a thin smile. "When you have been here in Westbury Park a little longer, you will learn that there are very few things which can be kept secret," he said.

"There's one secret nobody seems to know the answer to," Woodend countered, "who the bloody hell killed Gerhard Schultz? Anyroad, to get back to my question, it doesn't matter what Mr Rozpedek told me – I'm askin' *you* what you did when you got back to his house."

"We played cards."

"An' what game did you play exactly? Was it snap? Or are you more inclined towards happy families?"

"We played poker," the young Pole said. "I lost seven shillings and elevenpence."

Woodend scratched the edge of his nose with his index finger. "It's always fascinatin' to me how people who don't know any better think that addin' little details to the story they tell the police will give those stories an aura of authenticity," he said. "Tell me, how long did it take you to lose your seven shillin's an' elevenpence?"

"It took me until long after Herr Schultz had been beaten to death in the woods."

Woodend sighed. "Just answer the question, please."

"The poker game went on until at least four thirty in the morning. It may even have been five o'clock."

"Were you all drinkin' as well?"

"Of course we were drinking. We are Poles. When there are three or four of us together, it is impossible *not* to drink."

"Then you must have had thick heads when you turned up for work the next mornin'. I'm surprised your foreman didn't notice anythin' an' report you to his supervisor."

Wasak shook his head, as if he despaired at the depth of the chief inspector's ignorance.

"We are all shift workers in a chemical plant which operates around the clock," he said. "Often we have to work at the weekend, and when that happens we are given time off in lieu. This was one such occasion. There was no work for any of us the day after Schultz was murdered."

"So between about quarter past eleven an' four thirty in the mornin' – or it might have been five o'clock – you were all together?"

"That's right."

"And nobody left durin' that time?"

"As far as I can remember, we all went to the lavatory at some point during the game."

They were hard work, these Poles, Woodend thought. It wasn't that they were all as thick as two short planks, just that they acted as though they were.

"You all went to the bog, but nobody was gone more than a couple of minutes. Is that it?" he said, spelling it out.

"Yes, that is correct."

The chief inspector rose to his feet. "Well, if you'll excuse me, Mr Wasak, there's a drink waitin' for me on the bar," he said. "By the way, who won this gin rummy game of yours?"

"Poker," the Pole corrected him. "Zbigniew was the big winner. And it was poker."

"Aye, so it was," Woodend agreed.

He walked back to the bar, aware of the eyes on him once again. Bob Rutter, who had already started to sip his own half of bitter slid a brimming pint over to his boss.

"Did you find out anything useful from your little chat, sir?" the sergeant asked.

Woodend shook his head. "I get the

distinct impression that at least half the people livin' on this camp don't give a toss whether or not I find Gerhard Schultz's killer," he said. "An' what's even worse, about half of the rest would much rather I didn't."

Rutter lit up one of his cork-tipped cigarettes. "That's hardly surprising, is it?" he asked. "Being a time-and-motion man has never been the most popular occupation in the world."

"True enough," Woodend agreed. "You know what's really got me foxed, Sergeant?"

"No. What?"

"This whole Dark Lady business."

"You mean you think there really might be a ghost?"

"No, course I don't think that. But what I want to know is why even the mention of this particular spook should have put the wind up Gerhard Schultz."

"Maybe he did believe in ghosts," Rutter suggested. "Maybe he was scared to death of them."

"So, bein' scared to death, he goes wanderin' off on his own in the dark?" Woodend asked sceptically. "Besides, I think you're forgettin' exactly how that Simon Hailsham feller phrased it. He said that it was when he first mentioned the Dark Lady that Gerhard Schultz was worried. As soon as he'd explained that she was nothin' but a local ghost, the German calmed down."

"So you're saying that Schultz must have thought the words applied to something else?"

"Exactly."

"But what?"

"He hadn't read his Dickens, but maybe he was a Shakespeare fan," Woodend speculated.

"A Shakespeare fan?" Rutter repeated, mystified. "What's Shakespeare got to do with this?"

Woodend shook his head in mock disgust. "You young coppers amaze me sometimes," he said. "For all your fancy grammar-school education, you still know bugger all. Shakespeare wrote a lot of sonnets – that's like limericks, only with more lines."

Rutter made a wry, long-suffering face. "Thank you for putting me right on that point, sir."

"He was married, as you probably know, to a woman called Anne Hathaway, but a lot of these poems were written to a woman who wasn't exactly his wife. Well, over the years she's come to be known to the people who've studied him as his Dark Lady."

"I don't see where this is leading us," Rutter confessed.

"Say Gerhard Schultz had a woman in his

past who he thought of as *his* Dark Lady – a woman he'd treated badly, an' either felt guilty about or was afraid of. When Simon Hailsham mentions the name, Schultz thinks that's who he's talkin' about, an', naturally, he's very shocked. Then he realises it's only a local legend that Hailsham's talkin' about, an' he calms down immediately. How does that strike you as an idea?"

"It's a possibility I wouldn't be willing to dismiss out of hand," Rutter said cautiously.

The chief inspector took a gulp of his beer. "I like havin' you around on an investigation, lad," he said. "An' there's two main reasons for that. The first one is that you're a good person to bounce ideas off. The second is that when I let my enthusiasm for a theory send me in chargin' off in all directions at once – an' don't deny it, lad, because I do..."

Rutter grinned. "Quite honestly, it would never have occurred to me to deny it, sir."

Woodend frowned, but only for a second. "When I let my enthusiasm run away with me, you're there to pull me back. So we make a bloody good team – an' we've got the results to prove it – but it looks like we're goin' to have to split up on this case."

"I beg your pardon, sir?"

"There's a strong possibility that the killer

is local. Not poor old Fred Foley – though where he's disappeared to is a mystery in itself – but somebody from the camp. He could be one of the Italians, like I said to Bernadelli. Or one of the Poles. But this whole Dark Lady business has got me thinkin', an' I've realised the murderer could just as easily be somebody out of Schultz's past. Somebody he knew down in Hereford, for example. An' that's our problem, you see. We don't really know anythin' about his past."

"So you want me to go down to Hereford?"

"It's either that, or leave it up to the local Mr Plods," Woodend said. "An' I've a lot more confidence in you than I have in them."

Rutter grinned again. "I don't know if you intended it, but that was almost a compliment."

"Aye, it was – *almost*," Woodend agreed. "An' I did intend it. But don't get too cocky, lad, because I'll certainly not be makin' a habit of it." He knocked back the remains of his beer, and stood up. "I think I'll go for a walk before I turn in for the evenin'."

It was a mild summer night, and though the moon was on the wane, there was sufficient light for Woodend not to need a torch. He walked through the park, looking at the curtained windows and wondered, as he often found himself doing in situations like this one, about the secret lives which were acted out once front doors had been firmly closed. He reached the edge of the park and turned on to the country lane which led to the main road which, in turn, eventually led to the town of Maltham.

It was then he saw it.

It was standing perfectly still no more than a hundred yards from him, in the direction of the canal. It was a bloody big horse, he thought, a fact which only served to make the cloaked figure sitting on its back look even smaller and more fragile than she probably was.

Making as little noise as he possibly could under the circumstances, he began to walk rapidly up the lane. He covered the first ten yards, then ten more. He heard the horse snort, but neither it nor its rider moved. He wished he'd brought a torch with him after all, but it was too late to go back for one now.

In the woods on either side of him, he could hear the noises of the night – the rustling as small furry creatures made their way through the grass, the hissing and buzzing of insects, the chirping of the crickets.

He had left the park well behind him, and with it all outward signs of the modern world. He could, with just a tiny leap of the imagination, picture himself in a very different world, one in which everyone knew their place – just like in the hymn – from the farm labourers in their simple hovels to the rich landowners up at the big house.

But Sir Richard Sutton had apparently not known *his* place in the established order. He had strayed from the path, bringing feelings of betrayal and humiliation down on his poor wife's head. And he had paid the price for that. But then, so had she. Two lives had been wasted that terrible night, and now, a hundred and fifty years later, there had been a third death – not more than a few minutes' walk from the place in which the first tragedy had taken place.

He was less than forty yards from the horse and rider now, yet they maintained their frozen tableau. Did the rider know he was approaching? And if she did know, did she care?

He could see that she was wearing a three-cornered hat, and though he couldn't swear to it, he was almost sure that a long mane of hair spilled over her shoulders.

At thirty yards the tableau was suddenly shattered, and the horse began to trot towards the canal.

But there were no hoof beats! Woodend thought as he broke into a run. Why were there no bloody hoof beats?

The horse was, by its own standards, going at no more than an amble, but the gap between it and the policeman was perceptibly widening.

"Stop!" Woodend gasped. "Stop! I want to talk to you."

The rider gave no sign of having heard him, but stayed as erect and silent in the saddle as she had done from the moment he had noticed her. Knowing it was probably pointless, Woodend put on an extra spurt, which made it all the worse for him when he stepped on something slippery and went sprawling forwards in the road.

He held out his hands to break his fall, and felt the shockwaves travel up his arms as his palms made contact with the asphalt. It took him a second or two to recover, and by the time he had pulled himself to his feet again, horse and rider had vanished.

Six

The morning sun was streaming in through the breakfast-room window when Woodend sat down at the only table which had been laid. There seemed to be no one around, but next to one of the serviettes was a small brass bell.

For a few moments the chief inspector sat staring at it, reluctant to use anything as imperious as a bell to summon anyone to serve him. Then he felt a pang of hunger, and decided it was not for him to buck whatever system they chose to use in Westbury Hall.

He rang the bell, and almost immediately Tony the bar steward appeared through the kitchen door.

"Good God, lad, don't you ever sleep?" Woodend asked.

Tony grinned. "We never have more than three or four people stayin' here at any one time," he said, "so it's not really worth

104

employin' an extra pair of hands." He tilted his head to one side, and examined Woodend with a professional caterer's eye. "I may be wrong about this, but you look like the full-cooked-breakfast type to me, Mr Woodend."

"You're not wrong. In fact, you're spot on."

"How would two eggs, sausage, bacon, tomato, mushrooms and fried bread suit you?"

"It'd suit me grand," Woodend said. "An' if you could find me some black puddin' from somewhere, I'd be your slave for life."

"I'll see what I can do for you," Tony said. "You like your tea strong, I take it?"

"So you can stand your spoon up in it," Woodend replied. "An' I'd like it in a big mug, if you've got one."

Tony nodded. "That's what I figured," he said, and disappeared into the kitchen again.

Woodend lit up a Capstan Full Strength, and got that jolt which only the first cigarette of the day gave him. It seemed remarkable to him that it was less than twenty-four hours since he'd got off the train, because, as with so many of the cases he'd worked on in the past, he'd already immersed himself in the small world in which the murder had taken place.

Westbury Park was now his reality, where-as London – which had been his home for nearly fifteen years – was nothing more than a distant dream, a vague memory of a time which used to be. And he had not even begun to scratch the surface of the park yet, he recognised. But before he finally left it, he would probably know more about the lives of some of the people in it than even their closest neighbours could guess at.

The kitchen door swung open, and Tony appeared, carrying a plate high in the air, as if he were delivering a feast. And to Wood-end, he was. The egg yolks looked soft enough to dip his sausage in, without being runny. The bacon was crisp and appetising. And there was black pudding. The chief inspector picked up his knife and fork, and attacked his breakfast with gusto.

He was just washing down the last of the bacon with his second mug of tea when Rutter entered the room with several news-papers in his hands.

"You wouldn't think it would make much of a difference where in the country you eat a fry-up, would you?" Woodend asked. "But it bloody well does. The only place south of the River Trent you can get food as good as this is in Joan Woodend's kitchen."

But Bob Rutter, it seemed, was in no mood to cross swords with his boss over the respective merits of northern and southern cooking. With an uncharacteristically dramatic gesture, he slammed the newspapers down on the table.

"Look at this bloody lot!" he said.

Woodend glanced down at the headline in the *Daily Mirror*: "The Curse of Lady Caroline".

He put it to one side, and read what the *Daily Express* had to say: "The Dark Lady's Ride of Death".

He chuckled. "That young woman from the *Maltham Guardian* told me she'd get the story in all the nationals, an' bugger me if she hasn't gone an' done just that."

"You're not angry?" Rutter asked incredulously.

Woodend picked up the *Daily Mail*, which proclaimed "New Twist to Age Old Mystery" and had the byline "Elizabeth Driver".

"You've got to admire the lass's spirit of enterprise an' determination, haven't you?" he asked.

"Have I?" Rutter countered.

Woodend shook his head, almost mournfully. "Sometimes I think you're more middle-aged than I am, lad."

"But don't you see what this will mean?" Rutter demanded. "We'll have busloads of people coming up here now. You'll not be able to move for busybodies on the lane at night."

"Well, that'll certainly make things a lot more difficult for her," Woodend mused.

"For who?"

"The Dark Lady."

It was Rutter's turn to shake his head. But in his case it was with amazement. "You've surely not started believing in this ghost of Lady Caroline Sutton, are you, sir?"

"There's often a lot more to these old legends than first meets the eye," Woodend said enigmatically. "What time did you say your train down to Hereford was leavin', lad?"

"I didn't," Rutter answered, still stinging from the implied rebuke about middle age. "But, as a matter of fact, it leaves Maltham in forty-five minutes."

"Then you'd better grab a decent cup of tea while you've got the chance, because personally, I wouldn't use that stuff they serve up on British Railways for weedkiller."

Woodend was hiding something, Bob Rutter thought. It couldn't be important, or he'd have shared it with his trusted sergeant – but he was definitely hiding *something*.

"What will you be doing with yourself while I'm away down south, sir?" he asked.

"Me?" Woodend replied, so innocently that it was almost a confession. "I'll be workin' my way down the list of people who were in the bar the night Gerhard Schultz was killed."

"Anything else?" Rutter persisted.

Woodend gave him a wide grin, an acknowledgement of the fact that he'd been caught out.

"Well, if I do find I have a bit of spare time on my hands, I just might go chasin' after the Dark Lady," he admitted.

Woodend had noticed Kurt Müller's sharp, intense features before, but the German had been sitting at a table in the club so Woodend hadn't really been able to see the man's hands. Now, standing in the doorway of the Müller's home, he noticed they were long and artistic – hardly the hands he would have expected to belong to a production worker.

"Yes?" the German said, as if Woodend were a complete stranger to him, rather than someone who'd addressed his group on the small matter of Gerhard Schultz's murder the night before.

"As I explained yesterday, I'll be interviewin' everyone who saw Mr Schultz just before his death," Woodend said.

"Yes, I remember."

This was as bad as dealing with the Poles, Woodend thought. "So that's what I'm here for now," he explained. "To interview you."

A thin smile came to the German's lips. "I hadn't expected you so soon. Both alphabetically and geographically, I should have been a long way down your list; yet here you are, only a few hours after starting your investigation, standing on my doorstep with your questions. So exactly what system are you using, Chief Inspector Woodend?"

I'm usin' the system of talkin' to the men who matter – the men who are most likely to know what *I* want to know – an' we're both well aware of that, Woodend thought.

But aloud, he said, "It's purely random, sir. I'm not a great one for organisation."

Müller's thin smile widened. "Then you would have made a very bad German," he said. "Please come inside."

The layout of the house was similar to that of the Bernadelli home, but the both the décor and atmosphere were totally different. The furniture had none of the cosiness of Mrs Bernadelli's. Instead, it was austere – a utilitarian cloth sofa, a heavy sideboard, and a plain carpet. The bookcase which stood facing the window was filled, not with paperbacks, but with what looked like weighty tomes. There were no ornaments, but on one wall hung a large iron crucifix, with two pictures of the Virgin Mary flanking it.

Woodend, with his Methodist background, shuddered at the anatomical exactitude of the crucified Christ.

"You're a religious man, are you then, Mr Müller?" he asked, when he'd sat down.

Müller nodded. "For a while, during the war, I lost my faith, but God, in His infinite mercy, has restored it to me."

"Were you a prisoner of war in this country?"

"No, my wife and I came to England together in 1946."

"Where are you from originally?" Woodend asked.

"Bavaria."

"That's where Gerhard Schultz came from as well."

"So I believe."

"Did you know him?"

Another thin smile came to Müller's lips. "It's said that if you talk to an Australian and say you come from England, he will be convinced that you must know a friend of his who lives only ninety miles from your home. You have fallen into the same trap as the Australians, Mr Woodend."

"Maybe you're right," Woodend agreed. "But you still haven't answered my question."

"True," Kurt Müller conceded. "But I will now. I can say in all honesty that Herr

111

Schultz was not brought up in my village."

"But since he'd been here, livin' in Westbury, you had met him, hadn't you?"

"As fellow Germans, we were introduced to each other in the bar by Mr Hailsham, the personnel manager. We exchanged a few words with each other. Nothing more."

"I get the impression you didn't like him."

"Then you are wrong. As I person, I didn't know enough about him to either like or dislike him. As he was a senior manager and I am a humble worker and we are therefore on different sides of the fence, I perhaps mistrusted him a little. As a German, I have to admire him for the part he played in the last war, even if his views differed from mine."

"Differed from yours?"

"I assume he believed in what he was fighting for, I didn't. But that's not the point I wanted to make. To have been a fighter pilot, to have faced the strong possibility of death every single day, demands a great deal more courage than I think I could ever have shown."

"Where were you at the time when Gerhard Schultz was killed?" Woodend asked.

"Here. With my wife."

"An' you didn't hear or see anythin' suspicious?"

"My wife was listening to the radio when I got home from the club. There was a concert on. It was Prokofiev's *Romeo and Juliet*, which has always been one of her favourites. I joined her on the sofa, because I know she always enjoys music more when I am listening to it with her. The concert finished at around a quarter to twelve, and that was the end of the evening's programmes, so we both went to bed. There could have been a dozen men murdered in the woods, and we would have known nothing about it."

"I assume your wife will confirm this."

"Of course."

"So could I speak to her?"

"She is not here. She works."

"As what?"

"She's a teacher in the local primary school."

"Is that so?" Woodend asked, wondering how Mrs Müller, as a member of the middle class, felt about having a husband who was a production worker.

"I have qualifications," Kurt Müller said, reading his mind. "I hold a degree in engineering."

"So why aren't you an engineer?"

"Because the work I do is not demanding, and leaves me time to think," Müller replied.

"So you're a bit of a philosopher on the quiet, are you, Mr Müller?" Woodend asked.

But the intense German was not to be rattled. "There are so many questions which need to be answered," he said. "The nature of God and the nature of the universe. Divine justice versus that justice which has been invented by man. I could live a thousand years – a hundred thousand years – and never find an answer. But at least I am making a start."

The man's sincerity was so obvious that Woodend began to feel slightly ashamed. Goading a pompous piece of work like Simon Hailsham was one thing; treating Kurt Müller's beliefs so lightly was quite another.

"I admire you for trying to understand," he said.

Müller's smile acquired a sad edge. "I am not quite sure that I'm worthy of your or anyone else's admiration," he said. "Do you have any more questions for me, Chief Inspector?"

Woodend stood up. "No, not for the moment." He gestured with his hand that Müller shouldn't bother getting out of his seat. "You stay where you are – I'll see myself out." He walked over to the door, opened it, then turned round again. "Oh, there is one more thing," he said.

"Yes?"

"I wondered if, as someone from Bavaria, the Dark Lady would mean anythin' to you."

Müller's eyes flickered, but only for a split second. "Why should you ask me that? What's it got to do with being Bavarian? As I understand it, the Dark Lady is nothing but a local ghost."

"An' you believe in ghosts, do you?"

"No, I don't believe in ghosts," Müller said. "But as a good Catholic, I do believe in demons."

The bar of the Westbury Social Club had just opened when Woodend got back to it, and there was only one customer – Mike Partridge, the red-faced balding man whom Woodend had identified the previous evening as the leader of the club's British contingent.

Partridge gave him a noncommittal nod, then returned to the serious business of studying his pint of bitter.

The chief inspector ordered his own pint from Tony and took it over to Partridge's table. "Do you mind if we have a word?" he asked.

Partridge looked up. With a face as red as his, it wouldn't always be easy to tell when he was getting angry.

"A word?" the production worker repeated.

"That's right."

"Or do you mean an interrogation?"

"You can call it an interview if that makes you feel any better," Woodend said easily.

"Why 'ere?" Partridge demanded. "Why 'aven't you come to my 'ouse, like you did with all the uvvers?"

The question offered a good opportunity to take the measure of Partridge's character, and Woodend grasped it with both hands.

"All the others – all the ones I've seen at their houses – they're foreigners," he said. "I wouldn't want to drink with them. But us English – well, we've got to stick together, haven't we?"

"I've nuffink against foreigners," Partridge said defensively.

"Neither have I," Woodend told him, winking. "Not as long as they stay where they belong – which is well an' truly in their own bloody countries."

"BCI don't encourage that kind of talk," Partridge said. "The way they look at it, we're all one big team."

"An' is that how *you* look at it?"

"Yes."

Woodend decided to try another tack. "Were you in the war, Mr Partridge?" he asked.

116

"I was."

"An' did you see any action?"

"I was wounded durin' the D-Day invasion. Got shot in the leg. They gave me a medal, but that don't do anyfink to take away the ache I get when the weather's damp."

"So because of a Kraut, you're goin' to be in pain for the rest of your life," Woodend said. "An' you're tryin' to tell me that you don't bear the Germans any ill will?"

Partridge shrugged. "I wouldn't 'ave 'Itler or Goebbels round to tea, if that's what you're askin'," he said. "But the way I've got it figured, the bloke who shot at me was just doin' 'is job. Bloody hell, I was shootin' at 'im an' 'is pals – what else did I expect 'im to do but fire back?"

He sounded very plausible, but Woodend was still not convinced. "How long have you lived in the park, Mr Partridge?" he asked.

"I don't live 'ere," Partridge told him. "I'm a single man, and all the 'ouses in the park are for married couples."

"Where do you live, then?"

"I've got a flat in Maltham."

"So why do you do your boozin' here?"

"It's where my pals are."

"An' how do you get here?"

"On my push bike."

"Must be four miles to Maltham,"

Woodend said thoughtfully. "That's an eight-mile round trip when you add it up. It seems like a lot of effort just for a couple of pints."

"The exercise does me good."

"Even with your bad leg? Tell me, Mr Partridge, where were you when Gerhard Schultz was murdered?"

"Probably somewhere between 'ere an' Maltham."

"Did you see anybody?"

Partridge shook his head. "At that time of night, there ain't many people about."

"Still, it would have been handy for you if a bobby had pulled you over for havin' no lights on your bike."

"It would have been 'andy, right enough," Partridge agreed. "but unfortunately, it didn't 'appen."

Woodend offered the other man one of his Capstan Full Strength, but Partridge shook his head and pulled a packet of thinner, cheaper Park Drive out of his jacket pocket.

"You're not from round these parts, are you, Mr Partridge?" the chief inspector asked. "From your accent, I'd say you come originally from the other side of London."

"That's right," Partridge admitted. "I'm from Southampton."

"So what are you doin' in Cheshire? Have you got family livin' up here or somethin'?"

"No," Partridge said cagily, and Woodend realised that this was the moment he had been attempting to steer the conversation towards – the moment he hit on something that the other man did not want to discuss.

"So why did you move?" he said. "Wasn't there any work in Southampton?"

"I expect there was if you were lookin' for it."

"But you didn't look?"

"It was like this," Partridge said. "After they'd patched up my leg an' I was discharged from the 'ospital, I felt like a change of air. So I came up 'ere. Does that satisfy you?"

"I don't see why it shouldn't," Woodend told him.

But he was thinking, I've heard some absolute bollocks in my time but that has to take the biscuit.

Partridge drained the rest of his pint and stood up. "If you'll excuse me, I 'ave to be goin' now."

Woodend nodded absently, but his mind was already off in another direction. Partridge came from Southampton. Hailsham's squadron, if it had fought in the Battle of Britain, must have been based somewhere in that area. All of which led to an interesting question – where, exactly, had Gerhard Schultz spent his time as a prisoner of war?

Woodend was already on his second pint when Inspector Chatterton entered the bar. The local man looked both harassed and frustrated.

"Caught Fred Foley yet, have you?" Woodend asked, although he already knew what the answer would be.

Chatterton shook his head. "It's like he's just vanished into thin air," he admitted.

"Him an' his mangy old dog," Woodend pointed out. "Anyroad, I'm glad you've turned up now, Tim, because I've got a couple of little jobs I'd like you to do for me."

The look of surprise on Chatterton's face spoke volumes. This was not like Woodend at all. He didn't ask for help – if anything, he devoted his energy to fending it off.

"It's not much I want doin'," the chief inspector continued. "Just a few inquiries. Normally, I'd leave it up to my keen young sergeant, but he's gone off to Hereford."

Chatterton did not seem to welcome the news. "BCI's got a plant in Hereford," he said, frowning.

"Aye, I know," Woodend replied.

Chatterton's frown deepened. "The company's very influential in these parts, sir."

"Yes, I've already gathered that."

"So you won't do anything which might offend the people in charge of it, will you, sir?"

Woodend sighed. "Look, I know it would be convenient for everybody round here if Schultz had been killed by poor old Fred Foley," he said, "but I don't happen to think that he was."

"Still, BCI is very conscious of its public image, you know, sir," Chatterton said.

"It must be," Woodend agreed, "or it'd never go around poisonin' half the countryside." He was getting bored with the way the conversation was going. "Let's get back to my little jobs," he suggested. "The first thing I want you to do for me is find out what you can locally about Mike Partridge."

"Shouldn't be any problem," Chatterton said, relaxing a little. "What was the second thing, sir?"

"What do you make of Simon Hailsham?"

"Solid enough sort of chap," Chatterton said. "Meet him sometimes at the Lodge."

"Oh, so the pair of you are members of the funny-handshakes brigade, are you?"

"Aren't you?" Chatterton asked, sounding surprised.

"Nay, lad. The last time I checked up on it, it still wasn't compulsory for a servin' bobby to belong to the Freemasons. Anyroad, I'd look bloody silly in an apron – an'

121

I'm not exposin' my right bollock for anybody," Woodend said. "But about this 'solid enough sort of chap' of yours. If it doesn't offend your fraternal feelin's too much, I'd like you to do a thorough background check on him an' all. Not his war record, I'll put young Bob on to that – but anythin' you can come up with that he's done since 1945."

The frown on Tim Chatterton's face had returned, and was now beginning to display ulcer-inducing worry. "Is there any particular reason for this check, sir?" he asked.

"Is there any particular reason I should tell you if there was?" Woodend retorted, with a harsh edge creeping into his voice. "You didn't ask me why I wanted a check on Partridge, now did you? An' far as I understand it, it's the role of local police forces to assist the Scotland Yard men workin' on their patch in any possible way they can."

Chatterton gulped. "Yes, sir. Of course, sir."

"Look, Tim, I don't want you to check on him for any specific reason," Woodend said, relenting his previous tone a little. "Half the time I do things, it's on a gut instinct. An' there's somethin' about Hailsham that just doesn't feel right to me. For a start, I don't like the way he's tryin' to drop this whole case in the lap of the Poles. An' I've got a suspicion that he might have known Schultz durin' the war – though I may be wrong on that. So just to get things clear in my own mind, I really would be grateful if you'd do what I asked."

"All right, I'll do my best," Chatterton said dubiously.

"Good lad! I knew I could depend on you."

"I really would tread softly with BCI, sir," Chatterton warned. "The company has powerful friends in high places."

"Don't worry, Tim, I always tread softly," Woodend said, "but I usually carry a big stick, an' all."

Seven

The senior staff canteen in British Chemical Industries' Hereford plant seemed to be constructed entirely of tinted glass and polished steel. As Bob Rutter ran his eyes along the metal counter and up the round metallic pillars, he felt as if he were in a spaceship – and then he realised, with considerable chagrin, that that was a very Woodendish sort of thing to think.

"We deliberately made the place very modern, you see," said the enthusiastic man who was sitting at the opposite side of the black glass table. "A thoroughly modern image for a thoroughly modern company – that was the thinking behind it. Certainly impresses our visitors from overseas, I can tell you that."

Robin Quist, the head of the personnel department in Hereford, had wispy brown hair and cheeks which just avoided being plump. He was younger than the sergeant had expected him to be, and considerably less self-important than his opposite number at BCI's Maltham plant. In fact, he seemed remarkably open and honest for someone in his job – though Rutter hadn't yet dismissed the idea that it could all be a front.

"The nosh isn't at all bad in here," Quist said, "and it's certainly cheap enough. BCI knows how to look after its workforce. Treat 'em well and you'll get the best out of them, that's our motto." He waved at a young blonde waitress who had just finished taking an order at one of the other tables. "Over here as soon as you like, Mavis my sweet."

The girl came immediately, and from the smile on her face it was evident to Rutter that Quist was one of her favourite customers.

"What do you fancy?" the personnel manager asked the sergeant.

"Whatever you recommend," Rutter replied.

"In that case we'll both have the soup du jour, and lamb chops with all the trimmings, Mavis my little love," Quist said. He turned back to Rutter. "Now we've got that little matter out of the way, how can I help you, Sergeant?"

"I suppose my first question should be: Did you know Gerhard Schultz for long?"

"I knew him for fifteen years, if you call that a long time. I was already here when he joined BCI."

"What was he like to work with?"

A frown came to Quist's face. It didn't look very much at home there. "Gerhard was very efficient," he said finally, "but..."

"But?"

"But perhaps a little abrasive," the personnel manager said reluctantly. "Still," he continued, brightening, "you have to remember it was just after the war when Gerhard joined the company, and men like him had been used to being in life-and-death situations where they expected their orders to be obeyed without question. My old boss, Arthur Fanshaw, was pretty much in the same mould. I just missed the war myself – that bit too young."

"Fanshaw was in the RAF, wasn't he?" Rutter asked.

"How the devil did you know that?"

"The personnel officer in Maltham said something about Schultz probably getting the job because he'd been a flyer. 'They shared the comradeship of the skies' were, I think, his exact words."

The soup arrived. "Mixed vegetable," Quist said with glee. "You may be right about Gerhard having got the job because he was another flyer – albeit one from the

126

other side. On the other hand, it may simply have been that old Arthur was half-cut when he hired him."

Rutter took a spoonful of soup. It wasn't bad, he decided. "So Mr Fanshaw had a drinking problem, did he?" he asked.

Quist shook his head. "Not as such. I mean, he liked his booze, but he knew enough to keep off it while he was in the office. It was only at night that he went out on the razzle."

The sergeant frowned. "But you just said he could have been half-cut when he hired Gerhard Schultz. Now you're telling me he never drank on the job. The two things don't add up."

Quist laughed. "Oh, I see what you're getting at. Gerhard was never actually interviewed in the office."

"He wasn't?"

"No. Arthur went down to London for some sort of conference. As soon as it was over, he headed for the nearest pub – which was just like him. That's where he met Gerhard, who was working behind the bar at the time – as a purely temporary measure, of course. Anyway, they got talking, Arthur liked the cut of Gerhard's jib, and the next morning he came into work and announced that he'd filled the vacancy for a time-and-motion man. That was the kind of chap he was – a real buccaneer. He'd never have got away with that kind of behaviour today, of course, but like I said, those were very different times."

"When did you take over from him?" Rutter asked.

"I was acting head of department when Gerhard arrived," Quist said, dipping a bread roll into his soup. "Far too young for the position, of course, but they needed someone to take over in a hurry, and I was on the spot. I've been lucky really. By the time the company got around to looking for a permanent replacement for Arthur, I'd already been doing the job – with a fair degree of success, I might say – for eighteen months, so the powers that be decided they need search no further."

"Wait a minute. What exactly happened to Arthur Fanshaw? Was he sacked? Did he resign suddenly or something?"

"Oh, didn't I mention that? A few days after he'd hired Gerhard, he was out on the razzle again, and he must have had too much, even by his standards. He staggered out of the pub, and straight under the wheels of a passing car. The driver of the car didn't stop. Well, you couldn't blame him really. I mean, it was Arthur's own fault."

"How do you know that?" Rutter asked. "Is that what the witnesses told the police?"

"There weren't any witnesses to the actual accident. It was getting late and the streets were practically deserted. But there were plenty of people who'd seen him leave the pub and were willing to swear he could hardly walk, so what other explanation is there?"

I can think of about a hundred straight off the cuff, Rutter thought, but then a bobby's always suspicious if everything isn't as clear as crystal.

"How long was there between Arthur Fanshaw getting killed and Gerhard Schultz joining the firm?" he asked.

"About a week," Quist said. "Gerhard was down in London winding up his affairs, so he didn't actually know that Arthur was dead until I told him the morning he arrived. Of course, he'd only met Arthur once, so it wasn't as much of a shock to him as it was to the rest of us. On the other hand, Arthur *had* given him his big chance, and he did seem genuinely upset to hear the news."

"Would you describe yourself as a friend of Schultz's, Mr Quist?" the sergeant asked.

The personnel manager weighed up his response for a few seconds. "I wouldn't really call us friends," he confessed. "I suppose the best you could say of our relationship is that we were amiable colleagues."

"In that case, if you could arrange it, I'd like to talk to some of the people who were his friends."

"Do you know, I've never really thought about it before, but now I put my mind to it, I'm not sure he had any real friends at work," Quist said, frowning again. "But if you like, I can ask around once we've polished off our meal. Apart from that, is there anything else I can do for you?"

"Do you happen to have Schultz's address from the time before he moved here?"

"Must be on the files somewhere. I'll get my Girl Friday to look it up for you. Very efficient young lady. Won't take her a minute."

"I'd appreciate it," Rutter told him.

Simon Hailsham marched into the bar of the Westbury Social Club with a look on his face which Woodend couldn't label at first. Then the chief inspector did find a name for it – the expression was one of triumphant malice.

"Thought I'd find you in here," the personnel officer said, making his words sound more like an accusation than a statement of fact.

"Can I do somethin' for you, Mr Hailsham?" Woodend asked, swivelling round on his barstool so he could look the other man squarely in the eye.

"It's more what I can do for you," Hailsham said crisply. "You see, while you've been sitting on your backside, drinking subsidised beer, I've been out solving your murder for you."

"Is that a fact?" Woodend asked.

"It most certainly is. I posted notices all over the plant, asking anyone who'd seen anything suspicious on the night poor Gerhard was killed to report it to me. And someone has. A man called Ted Robinson came to see me this morning. What he had to say was very interesting indeed."

"Which was?"

"Far better you should hear it from the horse's mouth. He should be here any minute now."

As if he'd been waiting outside for his cue, the door opened and an overalled man who was close to sixty walked into the room.

"I'm here, Mr Hailsham, sir," he said, unnecessarily.

"I think we'd better move to one of the tables," Hailsham said, shooting a hostile look at Tony.

"We?" Woodend repeated incredulously. "There is no 'we' in this matter, Mr Hailsham."

"I beg your pardon?"

"Let's get this straight right from the

start," Woodend told the personnel manager. "I don't let civilians sit in on my investigations."

"But if it hadn't been for me, you'd never have got to talk to him," Hailsham protested.

"An' if he turns out to be any use, I'll see you get full credit for findin' him," Woodend told him. "But, at the moment, what me an' Mr Robinson need is a bit of privacy."

"I see," Hailsham said. He turned and marched to the door, stopping only when he'd turned the handle, to add, "But be absolutely sure of one thing – you've not heard the last of this."

From behind the bar, Tony chuckled. "That's another pint I owe you," he told Woodend.

The chief inspector took a closer look at the man Simon Hailsham had brought to him. Ted Robinson's face was marked with the sort of lines which a man acquires only after a lifetime of feeling he's been badly done to by the world in general, and his eyes showed the cunning of someone who always knows where he can buy goods which have fallen off the back of a lorry.

The shift man licked his lips, almost like a dog does when it smells food. "I'm right parched," he said. "I could really use a drink."

"You amaze me," Woodend told him. "What'll it be? A pint of bitter? Or would you prefer a double whisky?"

"A double whisky."

Yes, Woodend thought, it'll always be double whiskies for you – as long as some other bugger is payin' for them.

They took the drinks over to a table in the corner of the room. By the time they reached it, the shift worker had already drunk half his whisky.

"Now what's this valuable piece of information you have for me, Mr Robinson?" the chief inspector asked, when they'd sat down.

"The night that German feller was killed, I went to a pigeon-fanciers' do at the Golden Cock in Maltham," Robinson said. "The pub'd got an extension on the licensin' hours, so the barman didn't stop servin' till midnight."

"Which means you'd probably had quite a lot to drink by the time they called last orders," Woodend said.

"I only had a couple of pints," Robinson answered, unconvincingly. "Anyroad, when I got out of the pub, I discovered my bike had got a flat front tyre. If you ask me, somebody had done it deliberate. Well, I couldn't ride it like that, could I? So I had to push it all the way home."

"Is this fascinatin' little tale of yours actually leadin' us anywhere?" Woodend asked.

"The point is, it must have been around half-past two when I finally got back here. My house is on the edge of the park, an' I was just openin' my front door when I saw them."

"Saw who?"

"Them Poles. Four of 'em."

"Which Poles?"

"I don't know all their names, but I do know that one of 'em was that Rozpedek feller."

Woodend took out his Capstan Full Strength. Ted Robinson looked hopefully at them, but after extracting one for himself, the chief inspector put the packet straight back in his pocket.

"So what were these four Polish fellers doin' when you saw them?" the policeman asked.

Robinson's cunning eyes sank to fresh levels of deviousness. "They were comin' out of the woods," he said. "All furtive-like, as if they'd been up to no good."

"From which direction were they comin'? Along the path that runs down to the lake?"

For a moment it looked as if Robinson were about to say, yes, that was exactly where they were comin' from. Then, with

134

evident regret, he shook his head and said, "No, they were comin' out at the other end of the park."

"Did you speak to them?"

"I did not," Robinson said emphatically. "I like to keep away from the likes of them as much as possible, thank you very much."

"Did they see you?"

"No, I don't think they did."

"So you saw them, but they didn't see you. Now that is what I call convenient."

"It's the plain truth I'm tellin' you," Robinson said. "They were out in the open, under the moon, so they were easy enough to spot, but me, I was standin' in a dark doorway."

"So what happened after they came out of the woods?"

"They stood whisperin' together for a couple of minutes, an' then they went their separate ways."

Woodend leaned back in his chair. "There's one thing that's been puzzlin' me right from the start of your story, Mr Robinson," he said.

"An' what's that?"

"Why did you wait until now to come forward with this valuable information of yours?"

The shift worker looked lost for an answer. "I didn't think it had anythin' to do with the murder," he said finally.

"You saw four men comin' out of the woods where the body was found the next mornin', and you didn't think it had anythin' to do with the murder?"

"Like I told you, they came from a different part of the woods," Robinson said sulkily.

"All right, let's say I accept that," Woodend said. "What's made you change your mind now?"

Robinson licked his lips again, though this time, Woodend suspected, it was more through worry than anticipation.

"I saw the notice Mr Hailsham had put up all over the works," the shift man said, "an' I thought to myself that maybe what I saw might turn out to be important after all."

"An' when you talked to Mr Hailsham, did you tell him the same story that you've just told me?"

"Yes."

"*Exactly* the same story?" Woodend persisted "He didn't ask you to change it at all?"

"How do you mean?"

"Well, for example, you could have said you'd seen four figures comin' out of the woods, but that you didn't recognise them, an' he could have persuaded you that they were probably the Poles."

"No, there was none of that. I know what I saw, an' I don't care whether you believe me or not, because I've already got the..."

"Got the what?"

"Nothin'," Robinson said sullenly.

"You can go now," Woodend said.

"That's it?" the shift man asked.

"You were expectin' somethin' else?"

"Well, I rather thought you might thank me for my help."

Woodend sighed. "On behalf of both Scotland Yard an' the Mid-Cheshire police force, not to mention the friends an' relatives of the victim of the crime, I would like to express our appreciation for your help in this matter."

"Yes, well, that's all right then," Robinson said, standing up and walking to the door.

Woodend watched him go. Even if the man had, in fact, seen what he claimed to have seen, it wouldn't take a halfway decent lawyer more than a couple of minutes of questioning him on the witness stand to destroy whatever dubious value his testimony might have.

Eight

It was a warm, sunny afternoon, and there was that special summer softness in the air which seemed to make living through the rest of the year of English weather all worthwhile.

Woodend walked down Elm Street, oblivious to the watching eyes from behind the curtains. He was wondering what it would be like to be a shift man – to start work at around dawn one week, in the early afternoon the next, and just before it was most people's bedtime the week after that. He himself had sometimes worked through the night on investigations, but always with the knowledge that once the case was cracked, once the murderer was arrested, his body would be allowed to return to its natural rhythms. For the shift men, that was true only briefly – when they got their days off in lieu. For the rest of time, they lived in a strange world out of step with the rest of humanity. And the chief inspector couldn't help thinking that, in the end, it was bound to turn them all a little peculiar.

Just ahead of him lay Zbigniew Rozpedek's house. Woodend knocked on the door. The Pole answered almost immediately, but when he saw who had come calling, his face went red with rage.

"I would expect this kind of harassment from the authorities if I was living under the jackboot of those communist bastards who run Poland nowadays, but I do not expect it in England," he said.

"When in doubt, go on the attack, eh?" Woodend said dryly. "That tactic didn't do the Polish cavalry a lot of good, did it?"

Rozpedek made tight balls of his fists. "If you weren't a policeman..." he growled.

"But I *am* a policeman. Can I come inside, please, Mr Rozpedek?"

"I do not want you in my house."

The chief inspector shrugged. "In that case, it looks like we'll be havin' our conversation down at Maltham police station."

"You can do that?"

"Oh yes. Even in England, the police still have some powers."

The Pole took an angry step back. "Then it would seem that I have no choice but to let you come in," he said.

Woodend followed the other man into his

living room. Rozpedek did not invite him to sit down, and when he poured himself a vodka from the unlabelled bottle, he did not ask Woodend if he would like one too.

"You were seen the other night. Did you know that?" the chief inspector asked.

"Seen?" Rozpedek repeated. "Seen where?"

Woodend sighed deeply. "You're not goin' to make this easy for me, are you? All right. We'll play it your way, if that'll make you any happier. On the night Gerhard Schultz was murdered..." He paused. "You do remember that night, don't you?"

"Yes, I remember it."

"On the night Gerhard Schultz was murdered, you an' your mates were seen comin' out of the woods."

Rozpedek knocked back his shot of vodka. "Who is making these accusations against me?" he demanded.

"It doesn't really matter who the people are, does it?" Woodend countered. "The fact is, that you were seen."

A sudden smile came to the Pole's face, as if he had just worked something out.

"Who the *people* are?" he repeated. "I do not think we are talking about *people* here. If you had more than one witness, you would not be playing this so close to your chest. And what is the value of only one witness.

140

He says that he saw us coming out of the woods, and we say we were not there. It's one man's word against four."

"Four?" Woodend said. "I told you the witness had seen you an' your mates. I don't remember sayin' how many mates."

"There were four of us playing cards. However many of us he claims to have seen, it is his word against ours," Rozpedek explained. "This witness of yours? Is he someone who works at the plant?"

"I'm not at liberty to reveal that information at the moment," Woodend told him.

"Of course he is from the plant," the Pole said contemptuously. "The only people who would be around the park at that time of night are those who live here. And that means he has to work for BCI. In which case, his word counts for absolutely nothing."

"Would you mind explainin' that?" Woodend asked.

"Certainly I will explain it. Mr Hailsham, the son-of-a-bitch who calls himself our personnel manager, had notices put up all over the plant asking for information about the night of the murder."

"I know that."

"Did you also know that he offered a month's wages to anybody who supplied that information?"

"He did *what*?"

Rozpedek smiled again. "A month's pay is a lot of money," he said. "I was tempted to go and see him myself, and tell him I'd seen the Germans coming out of the woods."

Fulton Crescent, which was where, according to BCI company records, Gerhard Schultz had lived for most of his time in Hereford, was a pleasant, tree-lined street of neat semi-detached houses. Bob Rutter walked up the path of the one next door to Schultz's old home and rang the bell.

The man who opened the door was around sixty-five, and was wearing carpet slippers and an old, ragged cardigan. A chap who didn't leave the house much by the look of him, Rutter thought – and therefore a good chap to talk to if you wanted information about the neighbours.

He produced his warrant card, and said that he'd like to ask a few questions about Gerhard Schultz.

"Oh him," the man said indifferently. "Got himself killed somewhere up north, didn't he? I read about it in the papers."

"How well did you know him, Mr ... ?"

"Dobson," the man supplied. "Edgar Dobson. How well did I know him? Hardly at all. We lived next door to each other for thirteen years, but we were never close. We

142

exchanged a few words over the garden fence now and again, and that was about it."

"But you must have formed some impression of him in all that time," Rutter coaxed. "There must be something you can tell me that will help me to build up a picture of the man."

"How do you mean?" Dobson asked.

Rutter sighed. From his experience, there were only two kinds of witness – the ones who would talk to you for ever if you let them; and the ones you had to play dentist with, dragging each word out of them like a troublesome wisdom tooth. Dobson plainly belonged to the latter category.

"Did Mr Schultz, for instance, spend a lot of time at home?" the sergeant asked.

"Not during the day."

"Of course not. He had his job at BCI. But what about the evenings and at weekends?"

"Yes, he was at home then," Dobson said. "He wasn't a great one for going out."

"What about his holidays? Do you know if he ever used them to travel back to Germany?" Rutter asked, remembering that all the guidebooks back in Schultz's room at Westbury Hall had been on places in Great Britain.

"I asked him once if he ever went home," Dobson replied. "He said he didn't. Said he'd had just about enough of Germany. Said he was perfectly happy to stay here in England. Can't say I blame him. After all, it is the greatest country in the world, isn't it?"

"What about Mr Schultz's friends, then? Did any of them come round to visit him?"

"Not male friends," Dobson said, his upper lip twisting with contempt as he spoke. "Not couples, either. He wasn't one for throwing noisy parties, I'll say that much for him."

"But he did have lady friends?" Rutter asked, picking up on Dobson's obvious disgust.

The other man snorted loudly. "If that's what you want to call them, then yes, he did."

"What would *you* call them?"

"I'd call them tarts," Dobson said. "There was a whole stream of them. Some would only be there for a couple of hours, some would stay all night. But however long they stayed, I knew what they were doing once that front door was closed. I complained to him about it once. Told him he was bringing down the tone of the neighbourhood."

"And how did he reply?"

"He told me to mind my own bloody business."

I'm not surprised, Rutter thought. "How

long did these girlfriends of his usually last?" he asked.

"I told you already, they weren't his girlfriends, they were nothing but common tarts."

Perhaps there was more to this than simple blind prejudice or sour grapes. "How can you be so sure they were prostitutes?" Rutter asked.

"Because I've seen a couple of them plying their filthy trade in the town centre. There was one I remember in particular – a big blonde woman who was almost as tall as Schultz was. Every time you go past Woolworths at night you'll see her – standing there in the doorway and waiting for her next customer to come along."

When Woodend entered the Westbury Social Club at just after seven o'clock, the first person he noticed was Elizabeth Driver. The journalist was sitting at the bar. She couldn't have been a member of the club, but she seemed to have persuaded Tony into serving her a gin and tonic. The chief inspector got the impression that when she really put her mind to it, she could persuade most men to give her anything she wanted.

Miss Driver smiled at him. "She was seen again last night. And not just by one person

145

either – there were several sightings."

"I assume that you're talkin' about the so-called Dark Lady of Westbury Hall," Woodend said.

"Well, of course I am. She rode up Westbury Lane towards the canal, then vanished into thin air."

"Maybe," Woodend agreed.

Elizabeth Driver took a sip of her drink. "How's the investigation going?" she asked.

"So far I've managed to narrow it down to the murderer bein' either a man or a woman, who could be young or old – or very possibly middle-aged," Woodend told her.

"You're making fun of me, aren't you, chief inspector?" Elizabeth Driver said, accusingly.

"No, lass, I'm just bein' honest with you. I have no idea who killed Gerhard Schultz."

Elizabeth Driver glanced at her watch. "Well, I must go," she said. "I've got deadlines to meet."

"A word of warnin', Miss Driver," Woodend said. "You should never forget that your job is to *report* the news."

The journalist smiled at him. "You mean, report the *news*," she suggested.

"I know what I mean," Woodend told her.

Gerhard Schultz's nosy ex-neighbour had

146

certainly been right about one thing, Rutter thought as he gazed from the other side of the road at Woolworths' doorway – the blonde woman certainly was tall. And since even at a distance he could see that she was wearing far too much make-up and had a slit up the side of her skirt which almost reached the top of her stocking, it looked as if Edgar Dobson had been right about the other thing, too.

Rutter crossed the road and walked past the woman, making a deliberately clumsy pretence of not noticing her. He carried on for a few yards, hesitated, then turned around and repeated the process in reverse.

It was the third time he passed her that she spoke.

"Are you lookin' for company, darlin'?" she asked, in throaty, seductive voice.

Rutter froze. "I'm ... I'm a married man," he stuttered.

The woman laughed. "You'd be surprised just how many of the men you see wanderin' around the town centre at night have a little wife waitin' for them at home," she said. "What they're doin', you see is lookin' for somethin' they can't get from 'er."

"And what might that be?" Rutter asked.

The woman licked her lips. "You know? A little bit of this an' a little bit of that."

147

"And ... er ... how much would a little bit of this and a little bit of that cost me?" Rutter mumbled.

"Two quid if you want it straight, an extra ten bob for anythin' special. Payable in advance."

Rutter put his hand in his jacket pocket. When he took it out again, it was holding not his wallet but his warrant card.

"Detective Sergeant Rutter," he said. "I am arresting you under the Street Offences Act of 1959. You are not obliged to say anything, but anything you do say will be taken down and may be used in evidence against you."

"'Ere, what is this?" the prostitute demanded. "Are you really a copper?"

"Yes, indeed," Rutter assured her.

"Well, you're not one of the ones from the local nick. I'd've recognised you if you was."

"I'm part of a special task force drafted in to stamp out prostitution," Rutter lied. "Have you been pulled in before?"

"Yeah," the woman said gloomily.

"How did it go? Did the magistrate just give you a fine, or did you serve any time?"

"The beak gave me three months last time."

Rutter nodded sagely. "In that case it could easily be six months this time. Unless..."

"Unless what?" the woman asked. She stamped her foot. "Oh, I see what this is all about now. You never intended to take me in. You just want a free shake, don't you?"

"No," Rutter said. "All I want is some information. Is there a café near here that's still open?"

"There's a Wimpy bar just up the road."

"Good," Bob Rutter said. "Show me where it is, and I'll buy you a frothy coffee."

Nine

It was ten fifty-three, which meant that the shift workers in the bar of the Westbury Social Club, had just seven minutes in which to order their last drink of the day. Woodend took a sip of his pint and looked around the bar. There was a fair crowd in the club that evening. Some of the faces were new to him, but there were others which were rapidly becoming as familiar as his own.

The Poles, for example. Despite the heated confrontation he'd had with Zbigniew Rozpedek earlier that day, they were all sitting at their usual table. Or perhaps it was *because* of the confrontation, he thought. Perhaps they were deliberately going out of their way to show him that they were not about to be intimidated – to demonstrate by their physical presence that as long as they all stuck to their story, there was nothing he could do to them. And they were right; it

150

was the word of four men against one witness. And it certainly didn't help that that one witness was a slimy character like Ted Robinson.

There were still many questions left unanswered in the chief inspector's mind. Assuming for the moment that it *was* the Poles who had killed Gerhard Schultz, why had all four of them gone into the woods after him? Surely two would have been enough? If they'd done it that way, the pair who were not involved in the killing could have stayed in Rozpedek's house, making a noise and moving about in front of the window to help establish their alibi. And even if they had decided it had to be the four of them – perhaps because they wanted to share the responsibility for the murder – why had they re-entered the park from a different side of the woods to where the body was found? Once they had done the deed, wouldn't they have wanted to get out of the woods as soon as possible, and taken the path, which was undoubtedly the shortest route? So … still assuming that they were the killers, what had made them go blundering through the trees with the blood of Gerhard Schultz still on their hands?

Woodend shifted his gaze to one of the other tables. Kurt Müller was presiding over the German table with quiet authority. The man was still a bit of an enigma, the chief inspector thought. He was deeply religious, but it didn't stop him having a drink. He was a qualified engineer, but preferred to spend his time on a boring, repetitive production line. And he seemed strangely detached from what went on around him – as if he'd learnt that the petty worries and cares which weigh down most people were of no real significance. Perhaps his sense of detachment stemmed from his religion, Woodend thought. When you were grappling with the complexities of the nature of God, you had little time left over to worry about pay rises and hire-purchase payments.

The chief inspector lit a cigarette, and made a mental note to see Müller's wife the next day and ask her if she could confirm his alibi, and shifted his gaze to the English table.

Mike Partridge, having cycled all the way from Maltham, was sitting with his cronies. He never looked happy, Woodend decided. He had none of the aura of tranquillity which seemed to hover over Kurt Müller. But there was more an absence of something about him – his red face and balding head made him an unlikely figure for a tragic hero, yet that was the impression he gave Woodend. Maybe Bob Rutter's inquiries in Southampton the next day would explain why.

He took another swig from his pint glass. Why had the Poles taken that route through the woods? he asked himself for the fiftieth time. Perhaps he would take a leaf out of Tim Chatterton's book and go and find out for himself.

He stood up, and would have headed straight for the door if he hadn't noticed that someone was missing from the Italian table.

"Why hasn't Mr Bernadelli come out to play tonight?" he asked the Italians who were there.

Two of the men grinned broadly at him, and the third actually sniggered.

"Maybe he has better things to do with his time," said the one who'd sniggered.

"Oh aye? Like what?"

"He is very good with his hands," the Italian said. "Maybe he's mending a broken chair – or stuffing a new cushion!"

The other men at the table, who had obviously had a fair amount to drink, found this comment so achingly funny that they spluttered into their beers.

"The big trouble with private jokes is that people who aren't in on them never get to appreciate just how clever you've been in makin' them," Woodend told the smirking man. "An' the big trouble with murder inquiries is that most of the time, they're not really very humorous at all. So I'll ask you again, shall I? Where's Mr Bernadelli tonight?"

The Italian's face assumed a mock-serious expression. "I really do not know, Mr Policeman," he said.

"But if he was not our friend, we might make a pretty good guess," said one of the others, giggling.

Bob Rutter ignored the knowing, slightly repelled look from the girl behind the counter, and took the two frothy coffees back to the table where the woman – who said her name was Roxy – was waiting for him.

Under the bright lighting, the prostitute's thick make-up appeared even more garish than it had out on the street. He took a closer look at her face. Her grey eyes had a hardness about them, her nose was quite a large one for a woman – almost, in fact, hooked – and her lips were perhaps a little too thick. Yet despite it all, there was no denying there was a strange attractiveness about her. Still, the sergeant found himself wondering just what kind of man would seek out her services.

Well, he reminded himself, there was

Gerhard Schultz, ex-fighter pilot and time-and-motion man, for one.

Roxy unwrapped her sugar cubes carefully, and dropped them into her coffee. She watched the bubbles which formed as a result, and only when they had subsided did she look up at Rutter.

"So just what was it that you were so bloody keen to talk to me about?" she asked.

"I'd like you to tell me everything you know about a man called Gerhard Schultz."

Roxy looked puzzled. "Never heard of 'im," she said. "Is he a foreigner, or somethin'?"

"That's right. A German. He used to live in a semi-detached house in Fulton Crescent."

"Oh, now I know who you mean," Roxy exclaimed. "I used to call 'im Adolf. Not to 'is face, of course."

"How did you meet him?"

"The first time, he picked me up outside Woolworths. Said he wanted me for the whole night. Well, I was glad to get the weight off me feet, if the truth be told, so I said yes."

"You went to his house?"

"That's right."

"And you had sex?"

The prostitute smiled wearily. "Not

155

straight away. He liked to play around a bit first."

Rutter was starting to feel hot under the collar. Cloggin'-it Charlie, he was sure, would have had no difficulty with this conversation, but then Woodend wouldn't have felt quite so much like a callow youth under this experienced woman's gaze.

"Er ... what do you mean when you say that he liked to play about a bit first?"

"He 'ad these costumes hangin' in 'is wardrobe. He said we should put them on."

She was teasing him, Rutter thought – taking pleasure in his obvious discomfort. But he supposed that was fair enough – he'd scared her earlier, and now she was getting her own back.

"What sorts of costume did Schultz have?" he asked the prostitute.

Roxy smiled again. "You men! Policemen and milkmen, doctors an' bus drivers – you're all the same when it comes down to it, aren't you? All you're really interested in is the juicy details."

Rutter was sure he was blushing furiously. "The details might be pertinent to the inquiries I'm conducting," he said – meaning it, but knowing that he was sounding unconvincing.

"Oh, that's why you're askin', is it?" Roxy said disbelievingly. "Well, there were only two. A corset for me – which was so tight it nearly crushed me bleedin' ribs, by the way – an' a uniform for 'im."

"What kind of uniform?"

Roxy laughed throatily. "Most men would be more interested in what kind of corset it was."

"Tell me about the uniform," Rutter said, running his index finger between his shirt collar and his neck.

"It was an army uniform. German, I suppose."

"Are you sure it was army?" the sergeant asked. "Or could it perhaps have been airforce?"

"I couldn't tell the difference."

"Did it have wings on it?" Rutter persisted.

"Can't say I noticed."

"Close your eyes and try to picture it."

Roxy shook her head. "That wouldn't do no good," she said.

"You don't know that until you try."

The prostitute sighed. "Yes, I do. The punter rents me body, but he doesn't rent me mind. Understand?"

"Yes."

"All the time he's puffin' an' gruntin' away, I'm not really with 'im. I'm thinkin' about where I'm goin' for me 'olidays next year or addin' up the Co-Op bill. So you see, you're lucky I can remember 'e was wearin' a uniform at all."

"What did you do when you'd put your costumes on?" Rutter asked, trying another line of questioning.

"He'd tie me to a chair, an' shout at me. Really rant, if you know what I mean. Sometimes he could go on for hours."

"What kinds of thing would he shout?"

Roxy laughed again. "Do I look like somebody who understands German?" she asked.

"So he shouted at you in German?"

"I imagine it was German he was speakin'. It certainly wasn't nothin' that I could understand."

What happened next?"

"He'd untie me legs – but not me hands – an' I'd stand facin' the wall, while he whipped me."

"Whipped you!" Rutter repeated.

"Only very light. There was no way I was goin' to get cut for a miserable five quid. Then, when that was over, we'd do the business. All the messin' around got 'im proper worked up. I 'ave to admit, he was a real tiger between the sheets. Once or twice I even enjoyed meself."

"How often did you see him?"

Roxy shrugged. "I don't keep a diary," she said. "It was probably about once a month over the last couple of years. Then he said he wouldn't be needin' me again, because he was movin' away."

"Did he ever tell you any personal details? You know what I mean. Did he ever confide in you when you were lying in bed together?"

"He wasn't one of them who needed to be conned into thinkin' it was a romantic evenin'," Roxy said. "He paid for 'is pleasure, an' he wanted full value for money."

"Did you ever meet any his friends?"

Roxy gave him a hard stare. "Listen, I may be on the game, but there's some things that even I draw the line at, an' three in a bed is definitely one of them."

"I didn't mean that," Rutter said hastily. "All I was asking was whether any of his friends called at the house while you were there."

"No."

"And he didn't mention any names. Like Simon Hailsham? Or Mike Partridge?"

"I told you, it was strictly business with 'im. I could turn 'im on in bed without askin' 'im what he wanted, but apart from that, I don't know any more about 'im now than I did when he first picked me up outside Woolies."

It was half an hour past midnight as Wood-end made his way though the park, but there were lights on in at least a third of the living rooms, no doubt because men who had come off the ten o'clock shift wanted to grab a couple of hours' relaxation before turning in for the night.

When the chief inspector reached the edge of the woods – the edge from which Ted Robinson claimed he had seen the Poles emerging – he switched on his torch. The closest tree was lit up almost as if it were day, but the ones beyond the edges of the beam were little more than ominous black shapes. Woodend lit a cigarette for company, and stepped into the woods.

He did not know which direction to strike out for, so he chose the course of least resistance, walking in a straight line until he encountered the brambles of a rhodo-dendron bush, then veering off to either the left or the right. Around him, tiny insects buzzed. In the distance, an owl hooted. But other than that, the wood was silent.

He wondered how far he was from the lake. And how easy it was going to be to find his way back to the park. Perhaps, like Hansel and Gretel, he should never have entered the enchanted forest without first making sure that his pocket was filled with breadcrumbs.

He sensed that he was not alone in the woods just seconds before he heard the sound of a snapping twig. He came to a sudden halt, and swung his torch round in an arc.

"This is the police!" he said in a loud, commanding voice. "Whoever you are, come on out."

Nothing moved. No one emerged.

"This is a free country, an' you've a perfect right to be in the woods at this time of night," the chief inspector said. "So you're not in any trouble. I'd just like to know who you are."

Talk about an understatement, he told himself. I'd bloody *love* to know who you are!

From the other end of the woods, the owl hooted again and this time, because of what had happened since the last call, it startled him. He strained his ears to pick up the sound of a cough or heavy breathing, but there was nothing.

Who could it be out there hiding in the trees? And whoever it was, why the hell should they want to be out there?

He had three choices, he decided. The first was to stick to his original plan and carry on exploring the woods, as if nothing out of the ordinary had happened. The second was to beat a hasty retreat back to the safety of

Westbury Park. And the third? The third was to try to find whoever else was in the wood – which, given that someone had been murdered in this same wood less than a week before, was probably not the wisest course.

He strained his ears for sound of the man's movement – and whatever else he was uncertain about, he felt absolutely sure it was a man out there – but the silence still prevailed. He would have to be guided by the noise of the snapping twig he had heard a minute earlier.

It was, he knew from experience, very difficult to pinpoint noise in a wood, where sound bounces from tree to tree, but as far as he could tell, the man was hiding somewhere over to his left. Shining his torch in front of him, he took a cautious step in that direction.

He had covered no more than a few yards when the man jumped him. The assailant came up from behind, springing on to his back, and wrapping his arms tight around the chief inspector's neck.

He'd never have got me so easy a few years ago, Woodend thought, as the two of them hit the ground. I must be gettin' old.

His attacker rolled him over, and straddled his chest. Woodend felt a fist crunch against his left cheekbone. This bastard meant business – and, by Christ, he was strong.

The other man raised his arm to strike again. Woodend caught it at the elbow with both his hands – and twisted. His opponent screamed, then did a somersault which was so sudden that Woodend lost his grip.

The chief inspector struggled to his feet at roughly the same moment as his attacker. He looked around for his torch. It was lying several feet away, uselessly lighting up an area of the wood where nothing was going on.

The other man had raised his fists, ready for a fresh onslaught.

"Aye, come on, lad," Woodend said softly, taking up a fighting stance himself. "Let's see how well you do when you haven't got the element of surprise on your side."

His opponent hesitated for a second, then turned and fled deeper into the woods. The chief inspector followed, but had taken only a few steps when his foot caught against a root and he went sprawling forward.

"Shit," he groaned as he was lying on the ground. "Doesn't matter who you're chasin', Charlie – dark ladies on horseback or dangerous nutters in the woods, you always seem to end up fallin' over."

He picked himself up and dusted himself down. He would have a few bruises come the morning, he guessed, but apart from that, all he had suffered was a loss of dignity.

He rescued the torch and shone it on the ground. There were several footprints, some of his own and some which looked as if they'd been made by a size-eight or -nine heavy industrial boot. So no surprises there.

If his attacker had wanted to, he could have done a much better job of it, the chief inspector thought. Why jump on him when it would have been just as easy to hit him on the back of the head with one of the stones which lay readily at hand? And why, once he had chosen the former course of action, hadn't he followed it through?

Because he had suddenly lost his nerve? No, Woodend told himself, it wasn't that. His assailant had run away because the real purpose of the attack had never been to hurt – it had only been to distract. And for that night, at least, it had worked. He'd lost his appetite for exploring, and as soon as he could find his way back to the club, he'd go straight to bed.

He discovered he was limping slightly, but that would soon wear off. And it had been worth a few aches and pains to learn so much – because while he still didn't know what he was looking for, he was convinced it was out there, somewhere in the woods.

Ten

Woodend watched the tall silver-haired man in the expensive tweed suit hover on the threshold of the Westbury Hall breakfast room as if he had still not made up his mind whether or not to enter it.

A BCI man? the chief inspector wondered, as he speared the last remaining piece of sausage and popped it into his mouth. Probably – or why else would he be there?

The man had evidently made his decision, and walked over to Woodend's table.

"Do I have the pleasure of addressing Chief Inspector Woodend?" he asked, in a plummy voice.

"That's me," Woodend agreed. "An' you'd be ... ?"

"Howard Blake," the other man replied, and when Woodend didn't respond with recognition, as he'd obviously been expected to, he added, "for my sins, I'm the chief constable."

Bloody hell! Woodend thought. The chief constable. The feller his sarky minions called 'Sexton' Blake. What was he doing in Westbury Park at that time of the morning?

The chief inspector put down his knife and fork, and was starting to rise to his feet when Blake gestured him with his hand to sit down again.

"Let's not stand on ceremony, Mr Woodend," the chief constable said. "This is very much in the nature of what you might call a purely informal visit, so why don't you just get on with your breakfast while I have my say."

Blake took the chair opposite the chief inspector's. Woodend looked out of the window. There was no police car there, just an expensive Austin Westminster. There was no sign of a police driver, either.

Woodend sliced into a rasher of bacon as if that were the only thing which concerned him, but his mind was already in overdrive. Chief constables usually steered a very wide berth of him, and he was far from happy that this one had not only come to see him – when it would have been much easier to summon him to the station – but had come alone, in his private car, when there was unlikely to be anyone else about to see him. Worse still, he'd come out of uniform.

"You seem to have been in the wars," Blake said, looking at the bruise on Woodend's cheek.

"Aye, I walked into a door, sir," Woodend told him. "An' the bugger of it is, I was stone-cold sober at the time."

The chief constable's fingers played the table as if it were a piano. Drum, drum, drum. Drum, drum, drum.

He's nervous, Woodend thought. Now why the bloody hell should he be nervous?

"We ... er ... don't seem to have seen a great deal of you down at Maltham Central," Blake said.

Woodend dipped the bacon into his egg yolk. The chief constable was definitely rattled, he decided.

"You haven't seen *anythin'* of me down at Maltham Central, sir," he corrected Blake. "Hangin' around cop shops is not the way I work. Everythin' I need to solve the case is right here."

"Yes, I ... er ... appreciate that your methods are both slightly unconventional and usually highly successful, Chief Inspector..."

"Thank you, sir."

" ...but I was wondering if, in this particular investigation, you might have lost your focus a little."

Woodend sliced up his fried bread into

rough squares. "How do you mean, sir?" he asked innocently.

"Well, you see, I happen to have run into Simon Hailsham yesterday evening..."

"Run into him, you say? Would that have been in the pub? Or was it in the Lodge?"

Blake frowned. "It was perhaps the wrong choice of words," he admitted. "As a matter of fact, I saw him in my office."

"So it wasn't even in the least bit what you'd describe as a casual encounter, then?"

"He was most eager to talk to me," Blake said, ignoring Woodend's last comment. "It seems that the people at BCI are rather concerned about the leisurely pace at which you seem to be conducting your investigation. Of course, their concern is heightened by the fact that the newspapers, by tying the murder in to these ludicrous stories about this so-called Dark Lady, are generating a great deal of adverse publicity."

So that was why Blake was so edgy, Woodend thought – because he wasn't there in his capacity as chief constable, he'd come as the messenger boy for the mighty BCI.

"So I've been conductin' my investigation at a leisurely pace, have I, sir?" he asked. "I have been here less than two days. Just how soon are you expectin' me to make an arrest?"

"I don't expect miracles," the chief constable said defensively, "but from what I understand, there are some obvious suspects."

Woodend sighed. "Yesterday, everybody at Maltham Central was convinced a dosser called Fred Foley had done Schultz in," he said. "Now, suddenly, it's the Poles who did it. It seems to me that you don't really care who's charged, as long as somebody is. An' the only reason for such unseemly haste – as far as I can tell – is that BCI wants the matter over an' done with, so it can concentrate its full attention on makin' obscene profits."

Blake reddened slightly, but kept his temper under control. "The Poles have an obvious motive," he said. "It's well known that they hate the Germans in general, and they probably felt an extra antipathy towards Gerhard Schultz, since he was one of their bosses. In addition, they clearly had both the means and the opportunity. And if all that were not enough, there's a witness who actually placed them near the scene of the crime."

"If the witness is tellin' the truth, then they were seen at the other side of the woods from the spot where the murder took place," Woodend pointed out. "An' we don't know the witness *is* tellin' the truth – he

169

could have said what he did just to get the bribe from BCI."

The chief constable's flush deepened. "Bribe is rather a harsh word to use under the circumstances," he said.

"So which word would you prefer to use, *under the circumstances?*" Woodend asked, sounding genuinely interested.

Blake stroked his chin reflectively. "Financial incentive would, I feel, more accurately reflect the true position."

"All right, we'll call it that if it makes you feel better. But even with a witness spurred on by a 'financial incentive', we still haven't got enough evidence to charge the Poles."

"If that's your instinct, then I'm prepared to accept it," Blake said. "You see, I really am trying to see things from your point of view. But surely, if we were to arrest these Poles, and question each of them separately one of them would crack in order to save his own skin."

"Shall I tell you what I think?" Woodend asked.

"Of course."

"I think the Poles *were* in the woods that night – just like Ted Robinson said they were – but their purpose for bein' there had nothin' to do with Gerhard Schultz's death."

"So what were they doing?"

"I don't know – yet."

"Then pull them all in, and we'll soon have your answer for you!" Blake said, exasperated.

Woodend shook his head. "You don't know them like I do, sir. As far as they're concerned, it's them against the world. They're a really tight little bunch, an' they'd never admit to anythin' that'd get their pals into trouble. It'll be far better to wait until we've got somethin' definite on them. But whatever that somethin' is, I can assure you that it won't be a murder charge."

Blake had plainly reached the limits of his tolerance – or of BCI's tolerance.

"I would have expected more co-operation from Scotland Yard."

"An' I would have expected the professional courtesy of bein' allowed to do my job without interference, *sir*," Woodend countered.

Blake stood up so violently that he almost knocked his chair over.

"As soon as I get to the station, I shall be putting in an official complaint to your superiors about your attitude," he said.

"That's your privilege, sir," Woodend replied, mopping up the last of egg yolk with the last of his fried bread squares.

But he was more worried than he was letting on. There'd been a time, a few months earlier, when he had contemplated moving into administration. Then he'd realised just how important his current job was to him – how, in a way he wasn't quite sure he understood himself, it both drove and defined him. And every time he clashed with authority, he was putting that precious job at risk.

He still had some food left, but he had suddenly lost his appetite. He lit up a Capstan Full Strength and watched Blake drive away. He'd made some powerful enemies this time, he told himself, and if he was to come out of the whole business unscathed, he was going to have to catch his killer soon. But he wouldn't do it their way. He bloody wouldn't.

Rutter had taken the overnight sleeper from Hereford to Southampton, and a taxi from the railway station to the police headquarters, so it was just after eight o'clock in the morning when he found himself standing at the front desk and talking to the duty sergeant.

"Mike Partridge?" mused the sergeant, who was white-haired and probably nearing retirement age. "Can't say the name rings a bell with me, but this is a big city, you know."

"Could you get one of your lads to check

through the records and see if he's ever been in trouble?"

"No problem at all," the sergeant assured him. His eyes swept across the lobby, and settled on a slightly portly, middle-aged constable who had just come through the door. "Are you workin' on anyfink important at the moment, Horace?" he asked.

The constable shook his head. "Not really, Sarge. As a matter of fact, I was just planning to grab some breakfast," he said, his tone indicating he hoped that might still be possible.

"This young bloke's a sergeant from the Yard," the duty officer said, dashing the constable's optimism. "Wants to know if some geezer he's interested in has got any form down here. Take him down to the records room and show him the ropes, will you?"

"I'll be glad to," the constable said, without much conviction. "If you'd like to follow me, sergeant."

Rutter did just that. The two men went along a corridor and down a set of steps to the basement.

"Now, who's this villain you're interested in?" the constable asked, as he opened the door to the dusty records room.

"I don't know if he *is* a villain yet," Rutter told him. "But his name's Mike Partridge."

173

"Mike Partridge?" the constable repeated. "About my age? Red face? Moved up north after the war?"

"Yes, that sounds like our man," Rutter agreed. "Do you know him?"

"Know him! I should say that I do. Went to school with the bloke, didn't I? And we were in the same unit in the army. I'm sure he's not got form – if he had, I'd know about it." An idea came to his mind. "Tell you what – instead of us wastin' our time down here, why don't we go somewhere else and I'll tell you all about him."

"Good idea," Rutter said. "Is there an interview room somewhere we could use?"

The constable grinned. "Oh, there are interview rooms enough in this station, but I also find I do my best remembering in the canteen."

The woman who came out of the house on Elm Road, some fifteen minutes after Chief Constable Howard Blake had left Westbury Park in a huff, had a wiry frame and was dressed in a smart, two-piece costume. She was in her late thirties, Woodend guessed, and though she must once have been a pretty woman, she now looked completely washed out. Yet the chief inspector also detected great strength in her – the same kind of strength her husband had.

"It's Mrs Müller, isn't it?" he asked as she drew level with him.

"Yes, I am Gretchen Müller."

"An' I'm Chief Inspector..."

"I know who you are," the woman interrupted. "Everyone in the park knows who you are. What do you want with me?"

"I'd like a little chat."

The woman glanced down at her watch. "I have a bus which I must catch," she said. "I am expected at my school in less than half an hour. I am the one who has the keys."

"I never had any intention of holdin' you up," Woodend assured her. "We can talk on the way to the bus stop."

The early-morning sun was shining on them benevolently through a gap between the huts, but Woodend got the distinct impression that the woman felt cold – that, in fact, she always felt cold.

"Your husband told me that after he left the club on the night of the murder, he went straight home, where he found you listenin' to a concert on the radio," the chief inspector said.

"That's right. It was Prokofiev's *Romeo and Juliet*."

"He also claims he sat with you for a while, until the station closed down for the night, an' then you both went to bed. Are you what you might call a heavy sleeper, Mrs Müller?"

"No, I'm not," the woman said. "Since the start of the war, I have hardly slept at all."

"Long time to go without sleep," Woodend said. "But that's neither here nor there. The question I really want to ask you is this: if your husband had got up again an' gone out, you would have known about it, wouldn't you?"

"Yes."

"So you're sayin' that your husband never left your side from the time he got home that night until you left for work the followin' mornin'?"

"I am a Catholic," Gretchen Müller said.

"With respect, madam, I don't really see what that has to do with anythin'."

They had reached the bus stop. The woman came to a halt, turned to face Woodend, and deliberately looked him straight in the eye.

"I believe it is a sin to lie," she said, "and I swear to you now, by all I hold holy, that I know with complete and utter certainty that my husband did not kill Gerhard Schultz."

There was the sound of a vehicle engine somewhere in the near distance. Woodend looked over his shoulder, and saw that a red North-Western single-decker bus was approaching.

He turned his attention back to Gretchen Müller. "I didn't ask you to swear any oaths," he said. "My question was simply, were you with your husband at the time when Schultz was killed?"

The bus pulled up, and the woman mounted the first step. "I know that the answer I have already given would be good enough for my God," she said. "It should certainly be good enough for you."

Woodend stood at the stop and watched the bus head down the lane. He believed Gretchen Müller when she said her husband hadn't killed Gerhard Schultz. So why the bloody hell hadn't she given him a straight answer to a straight question?

Constable Horace Greenwood of the South-ampton police ordered a Woodendian-sized fried breakfast, and sighed with content-ment as he began to attack it mercilessly with his knife and fork.

"So you went to school with Mike Partridge, did you?" Rutter said.

"That's right. Only we didn't use to call him Mike – we called him 'Womme'."

"Why Womme?"

"His favourite phrase was, 'Wo' me, miss'. You must have been to school with kids like him yourself – kids who don't mind doing wrong but are buggered if they're going to be punished themselves as long as there's some other poor devil around to take the blame."

Rutter nodded, thinking of a boy in his class in school who'd been just like that.

"So you didn't get on?" he said.

"Not then. Nobody liked him at school. I didn't like him much after he left school, either – at least not at first. He got a job down at the docks, and ended up married to a lovely girl from up our street who went by the name of Dora May Fielding and—"

"I didn't know he was married," Rutter interrupted.

"Well, he's not now, is he? Anyway, you'd have thought he'd have been happy with that – a steady job, a nice little house, and a pretty wife who had a bun in the oven before they'd been married a year. But it wasn't enough for Womme. He started knocking about with a barmaid he'd met in one of the pubs down by the docks. Everybody was scandalised, but it didn't bother Womme in the least – he was having his fun, and that was all he cared about."

"When was this?"

"Just before the war." Constable Greenwood smirked. "You'll have been a baby at the time."

He wasn't trying to be offensive, Rutter thought. He was just stating an obvious fact.

"You said you were in the same unit in the army. Did you join up at the same time?" he asked.

"No, I signed up straight after Poland was invaded, but Womme didn't seem too keen on the idea, and because he was in what they called 'vital war work', he could probably have sat out the whole war in Southampton if he'd wanted to. He told me later that he didn't sign up because he couldn't bear to be separated from his wife and child – and to be fair to him, he did seem very fond of the little kiddie – but if you ask me, his real reason was that he wanted to be near his fancy piece down at the docks."

"But he did join up eventually?"

"Oh yes. Straight after his family was killed."

"They were killed? How?"

"The Germans dropped a lot of bombs on Southampton during the Blitz – important seaport, you understand – and one of them fell on Womme Partridge's house."

"I thought all the women – or at least all the children were evacuated from high-risk areas."

Greenwood shook his head. "They all had the *opportunity* to go – and most of them did – but it wasn't compulsory. Anyway, like I said, Mike joined up – and you should have

179

seen the change in him."

"I imagine he was shattered," Rutter said.

"Oh, he was, there's no doubt about it. But that's not what I'm talking about. It was like the Womme I'd known had never existed. This new bloke didn't try to shirk his responsibilities like Womme had done; he looked for new ones. If anybody needed a shoulder to cry on, they could always go to good old Mike. If you were short of a few bob, he'd help you out – even if it meant leaving himself short. And when it came to D-Day, he was a real tower of strength."

"In what way?"

"You have to have been getting ready to go into battle yourself to know what it felt like," Greenwood said. "We were all scared, but there's different ways of showing it. Some of us just had a dull ache in our bellies, a bit like indigestion. But there were others really shitting themselves. The lads with the bellyache tended to look down on the others. But not Mike. He talked to them for hours. He kept promising them they'd come through all right – and because it was him talking, they believed it."

"But not all of them did, did they?" Rutter asked.

"Course they didn't. It was complete bloody carnage on them Normandy beaches. Mike got shot himself." Greenwood paused to sip his tea. "I remember the last time I saw him. I went to visit him in the field hospital. He looked terrible. 'It's my fault they're dead,' he said. 'You can't blame yourself,' I told him. 'There's a war going on.' But he wasn't having any of that. 'It's my fault,' he kept saying, just like it was some kind of chant, 'and I'll never forgive myself.' That was the last time I ever saw him. By the time I got back to South-ampton, he'd been discharged from hospital and moved away."

"Whatever happened to the woman he was going out with?" Bob Rutter asked.

"Oh, her! I don't really know, to tell you the truth. She's certainly not still around here or I'd have seen her. I mean, you couldn't really miss her, could you. So maybe she moved back to her own country."

Couldn't really miss her? Moved back to her own country?

"Are you saying that she wasn't English?"

"Didn't I make that clear earlier on?" Greenwood asked, sounding surprised. "No she wasn't English. Must have come on one of the ships from Africa or the Caribbean or somewhere like that."

"You mean, she was coloured?"

"That's right," the constable agreed. "She was a real darkie."

181

Eleven

The Maitland Temple School of Riding stood in the centre of a large paddock. As far as Woodend could make out as he was approaching it, the entire property consisted solely of a wooden stable and an ancient caravan which had had its wheels taken off and been put up on bricks.

The chief inspector reached the caravan and saw that the word "office" had been written on the door in green chalk. He knocked. The woman who answered the knock was around forty-five years old. Her greying hair was tied back in a tight bun, and her face was reddened by much exposure to the open air. She was wearing a woollen sweater – which did little to hide her large breasts – and tan jodhpurs which served to emphasise her formidable rump.

She ran a critical – though totally asexual – eye over him. "It'll have to be one of our bigger horses if it's going to carry your weight," she said. "Still, it looks like you might have a good seat. Have you done any riding before?"

Woodend smiled, shook his head, and showed her his warrant card. "I'd like to ask you a few questions about Luigi Bernadelli," he said. "Assumin', of course, that I'm talkin' to Mrs Maitland Temple."

"Yes, I'm Polly Maitland. But it's Miss, not Mrs." The woman frowned. "Is this anything to do with the murder up at Westbury Park? Because if it is, you're barking up the wrong tree by asking questions about Lou. I've seen the way he works with my horses. You can tell a hell of a lot about a man from the way he handles animals. Certainly enough for me to say with absolute confidence that Lou wouldn't even tread on an ant if he could help it."

"I'm askin' questions about all the men who saw Gerhard Schultz just before he was murdered," Woodend said. "It doesn't necessarily mean I suspect any of them. So if you'd just spare me a few minutes of your time, Miss Maitland, I'd really appreciate it."

The woman turned the idea over in her mind. "All right," she agreed finally. "If answering your questions will eliminate Lou Bernadelli from your inquiries, then I suppose I can find the time. Come into my parlour, as the spider is supposed to have said to the fly."

Woodend followed her into the caravan. Inside it were crammed a battered desk, an equally battered filing cabinet, two straight chairs and two overstuffed armchairs.

"Take one of the comfy seats," Polly Maitland told Woodend. "But watch out for the loose springs."

While the chief inspector was gingerly lowering himself into the armchair, Miss Maitland went over to the desk and produced a bottle and two glasses from the desk drawer.

"Brandy," she announced. "Says it's French on the label, but at the price I paid for it, I'd be surprised if it had been anywhere closer to France than Algiers. Still, it's good enough for this time of the morning. Not too early for you, is it?" she concluded, giving Woodend a look which suggested that this was more a test of his manliness than a casual enquiry.

"It's never too early for a spot of *eau de vie de turpentine*," Woodend told her.

The woman raised a surprised eyebrow. "So you speak French, do you, Chief Inspector?"

"A smatterin'," Woodend said. "I picked it up durin' the war. Bit of German, an' all."

"Well, you *are* an unusual policeman,"

Polly Maitland said. She poured two shots of the brandy, handed one to Woodend, and plopped down in the chair opposite with a healthy disregard for the loose springs which she'd warned him about. "So what do you want to know about Luigi?" she asked.

"How long has he been workin' for you?"

"Strictly speaking, he doesn't work for me at all. Oh, I slip him the odd pound or two now and again—"

She stopped suddenly, as if she realised she'd said something she shouldn't have.

"It's all right," Woodend assured her. "I'll not tell the taxman."

Polly Maitland smiled gratefully. "You really are an unusual policeman. But as I was saying earlier, it's not the money which brings Luigi here."

"So why does he come? Because he loves horses?"

"Yes, that's right," Polly Maitland agreed.

But she had hesitated for the briefest of moments, and that hesitation was not lost of the chief inspector.

"What's his other reason?" Woodend asked.

Polly Maitland laughed. "Oh I suppose there's no harm in telling you of all people," she said. "You see, Luigi's a bit like a horse himself. Or, to be more exact, I suppose he's a bit like a stallion. Can't resist chancing his arm with the women when the opportunity arises. Even made a pass at me a few years back – and God knows, I'm no oil painting."

"You're sayin' he comes to the ridin' school because it gives him the chance to sleep with women."

"I've no doubt that's what he'd like to do if I let him. As it is, he has to content himself with letting his hands rove a bit when he's helping them on to their horses. Most of them don't seem to mind – he's a big handsome man, after all – but if one of them does complain, as happens from time to time, I tell her she must be imagining things, then give him a tap on the head with my riding whip to remind him that I'm not running a stud farm."

An idea too tentative even to be called a theory was starting to form in Woodend's mind.

"You wouldn't happen to have a list of all your clients, would you, Miss Maitland?" he asked.

Suspicion darkened the woman's eyes. "Now why would you ask that?" she said,

"Because if you have a list, I'd like to have a quick glance at it."

"I'm not sure I should show it to you," the woman said dubiously.

Woodend shrugged. "Why not? What harm can it do? There's no law against people takin' ridin' lessons, is there?"

"True," Miss Maitland agreed. "And after all, you are a policeman with a smattering of French."

She went over to the desk and returned with a leather-backed ledger. "This contains a record of all the people who've had lessons. It includes their names, addresses, telephone numbers and how many lessons they've had. But I'm afraid it only goes back two years."

"That should be long enough," Woodend said. "I don't think the person I'm lookin' for will have been havin' lessons for more than the last few months."

Then he opened the ledger, ran his eyes down the list, and saw almost immediately that was right.

The carefully tended gardens which surrounded the large detached house were so extensive that they almost qualified for the term "grounds", and Bob Rutter was finding it an extremely pleasant experience to wander through them with the white-haired man who carried himself so erectly.

"A large part of the Battle of Britain was fought in this area," the man said. "There might have been dog fights in the skies right above this house, for all I know. I could even have been in one – you don't look down to

187

admire the scenery when you're in the enemy's sights." He sighed. "I think that's probably why I bought this place – so I could stay close to those scenes of glory. And they were glorious, you know."

"I'm sure they were, Wing Commander," Rutter said, conscious, once again, of his relative youth.

"Since we didn't know when Jerry was going to be coming over, we had to be ready to be airborne for as long as the light lasted, and at that time of year that meant from four o'clock in the morning until ten thirty at night. We couldn't work a shift system – however fast they trained new pilots, we simply didn't have the manpower for that – so every flier had to be on duty at all times. It really was quite an exhausting business."

"It must have been."

"A lot of people have the wrong idea about our job," the wing commander continued. "They think we were supposed to shoot down German fighter planes."

"And weren't you?"

"No, we were supposed to knock out the bombers before they could do any damage." He looked up at the sky, as if he could see some even at that moment. "But of course, that meant dealing with the fighters who were escorting them first. And that wasn't easy. The German fighters – the 109s –

didn't fly alongside their bombers, you know. They flew above them, so that when we attacked the Ju 88s – that's the bombers – the fighters would come swooping down on us at a terrific speed. They had fuel injection, you see, so they could get away with it. If we'd tried a manoeuvre like that in any of our Hurricanes, we'd have stalled the bloody engine."

"There must have been a tremendous spirit of camaraderie in those days," Rutter said.

"Oh, there was," the wing commander agreed. "And in a strange way, that feeling extended to the opposition as well. We wanted to shoot their planes out of the sky, of course, but we never meant the pilots any harm. I remember one of my young chaps – his name was Chetwynd, if my memory doesn't fail me – being quite upset because instead of shooting the wing off an enemy plane, which was what he'd intended to do, he'd sprayed the cockpit and killed the pilot."

Which was pretty much what Simon Hailsham had said about his relationship with Schultz, Rutter thought.

"In fact," the wing commander continued, "I, and a few of my men, used to go and visit the captured German fliers whenever we got the chance. There was an internment camp quite close to the base, you see. The Jerries always gave us a very warm welcome – no hard feelings at all."

"Did you ever meet a German pilot called Gerhard Schultz?" Rutter asked, taking a shot in the dark.

"Schultz! How incredible you should mention him. Indeed I did know him. He was one of the prisoners I got closest to. An absolutely splendid chap. An officer and a gentleman in every sense of the word. I wonder whatever happened to him."

"You don't know?" Rutter asked. "Haven't you seen it in the papers?"

"Don't bother with the papers much any more," the wing commander confessed. "Got better things to do with my time than read about all the disasters going on in the world. Fought a war to make things better, and there doesn't seem to have been any improvement at all. So what's Gerhard been up to?"

"He's been murdered."

"Extraordinary thing to happen! Who on earth would want to kill a nice chap like Gerhard?"

"That's what we're trying to find out, sir," Rutter said.

And we might just be getting somewhere, he thought excitedly. We might – possibly – at last be establishing a firm link between the past and the present.

"You said you took a group of officers with you to visit the German prisoners, didn't you?" he asked.

"That's right. Not a big one. Just three or four chaps who were interested in coming along."

Rutter took a deep breath. "And did Simon Hailsham happen to be one of that group, sir?"

The wing commander looked blank. "Who?"

"Simon Hailsham. *Group Captain* Simon Hailsham," Bob Rutter prodded.

"Not done your homework properly, young man," the wing commander said severely. "That wasn't his name at all."

As Woodend walked through Westbury Park, he was thinking about his visit to the riding school and what he had achieved there. On the whole, very little, he decided. True, he'd cleared up one little mystery, even if he hadn't had time to bring it to its final resolution yet. And true again, he'd managed to eliminate one suspect from his list of possible murderers – but that list was still depressingly long. So all in all, it could hardly have been called a productive morning's work.

Even the expedition he was embarking on

at that moment was aimed more at getting the chief constable off his back than assisting him in catching his killer. But it had to be done. God, how he hated the politics involved in police work.

He entered the woods from exactly the same point at which he had entered them the night before. Once he had gone more than a few yards, however, he was no longer sure that he was still on the route he had taken the last time. Had he turned right by this bush? he asked himself. Or had he decided it would be easier to go to the left? After five minutes' walking he realised that any further speculation was pointless. If he was ever to find what he was searching for, it would have to be purely on a basis of hit and miss.

He had been walking for nearly an hour when he found an old brick building, not much bigger than a garden shed, close to the shore of the lake. An old pumping station, the chief inspector guessed, no doubt used to pump up water for the gardens and fountains of Westbury Hall when the place had been in its heyday.

The windows were all boarded up, and many of the slates on the roof were missing, but there was a shiny new hasp and padlock fixed firmly on the rotting front door.

"Did you have that idea of yours, an' *then*

go lookin' for a place like this, Mr Rozpe-dek?" he asked, looking around the empty wood. "Or was it the other way round? Did findin' this place give you the idea?"

Whichever way it was, one of the Poles had obviously been afraid he'd find the pumping station the night before, and had attacked him to stop him searching any further.

He hadn't known for sure that he'd need a screwdriver, but he was glad he'd brought one along anyway; because it saved him a trip back to the hall. He took the implement out his pocket, and inserted it into the groove of one of the screws which held the hasp in place.

Whoever had installed the lock had done a good job, and it took five minutes' work before Woodend could push the hasp to one side and open the door.

There was a good deal of metal inside the small brick room, but it was not the original machinery which had been used to pump water. The chief inspector examined the copper tubes with admiration. The Poles had done a first-class job, but then that was only to be expected. This was not a com-mercial enterprise – it was a labour of love.

It also explained why Fred Foley had hung around the hall so much, he thought. And how Foley's overcoat had come to be covered with the dead man's blood. But unless the Poles were hiding him – and he didn't think they'd take that risk – it didn't explain how poor, pathetic Foley had managed to evade the local police for several days.

Woodend closed the door again, and painstakingly replaced the screws. Then, whistling slightly off-tune to himself, he made his way back to Westbury Hall.

Commander Hartley Greaves of New Scotland Yard sat back in the leather armchair, took a puff on his expensive cigar, then reached for his balloon glass of very old French brandy. This club was something else, he thought – exclusive, expensive and downright classy.

He looked across at the man who was sitting opposite him and indulging in all this luxury as if it were no more than his natural right. Sir Roger Ives was around fifty. He had slim features and pale silky hair. At first glance, he looked mild and inoffensive, but his eyes, Commander Greaves had noticed right away, were as hard as diamonds.

Greaves took another puff of his cigar. He had been delighted to get the call from Ives – whom he had never met before – and had readily accepted the invitation to lunch, because when a man is approaching retirement age, it's always useful to start making contact with people who are in a position to find him a job which calls for very little work and a large pay packet. Yes, he'd been delighted – but he hadn't been at all surprised. Though no mention had been made of it yet, he was sure that the name of Chief Inspector Charlie Woodend would soon come up.

Even the thought of Woodend brought a bad taste to his mouth. The man was totally undisciplined. He dressed like a door-to-door brush salesman. He had absolutely no respect for people in authority – especially his own commander. He had developed sarcasm into an art form. And worst of all, he had the luck of the devil, so that while his approach to the cases to which he was assigned was all wrong, the bastard usually ended up solving them.

Sir Roger Ives flicked the ash on the end of his cigar vaguely in the direction of the ashtray. "We're experiencing a little local difficulty in one of our Cheshire plants," he said.

"Oh yes?" Greaves replied noncommittally.

"Yes. One of our chaps got himself murdered, and frankly, the senior officer you've sent up to deal with it seems to be making a hash of the job. There are some obvious suspects, but he seems quite content to let them remain at liberty. Not only that, but he practically accused one of our senior staff up there of committing the murder himself. Now we've tried to sort it out on the spot – the chief constable kindly agreed to go and see your man this morning – but it doesn't seem to have done any good."

Bloody right it hadn't, thought Greaves, who had wasted at least three quarters of an hour that very morning talking to Chief Constable Blake on the telephone.

"It's plainly impossible for us to deal with this man of yours ourselves," Ives continued. "That's why I was wondering if you might be in a position to help us."

Greaves took another deep, appreciative puff of his cigar. "You want me to take Charlie Woodend off the case?" he said.

Ives ran his right hand through his silky hair. "I would like you to do whatever is necessary to ensure there is a resolution to the case as soon as possible," he said. "If you decide that means removing the chief inspector, then so be it. It's a decision that only you can make, and I wouldn't dream of trying to influence you one way or the other." He smiled, but not with his eyes. "I hope that I've made myself clear, Commander."

"Very clear," Greaves said.

He paused. Make a favour seem too easy, he told himself, and it hardly seems like a favour at all.

"If it was left entirely up to me, I'd have Cloggin'-it Charlie on the next train back to London," the commander continued. "But if I pull him off the case after only a couple of days, there'll be questions, both from my bosses—" he pointed upwards; "and from the Police Federation—" he indicated the floor.

"I see," Ives said coldly.

"On the other hand, he has managed to get up the noses of some pretty important people," Greaves added, "and I don't see it will do anyone a lot of good to leave him up there *much* longer."

"What time scale are we talking about here?"

"If he doesn't come up with the murderer within the next forty-eight hours, I think I can put up a good case for having him replaced. Is that satisfactory?"

Ives nodded, slowly and thoughtfully. "Yes, I think we could safely say that would be satisfactory."

And then, when I've got Cloggin'-it-bloody-Charlie back in London, I'll do my level best to get the bastard kicked off the force, Commander Greaves promised himself.

197

When Woodend entered the Westbury Social Club just after two o'clock in the afternoon, it was to find a grim-faced Inspector Chatterton waiting for him.

"You've really upset the chief constable, sir," the inspector said.

"Do you know, I rather thought he might be a bit annoyed when he stormed out of the breakfast room this mornin'," Woodend said.

"According to his secretary, he's been on the phone to your bosses in London all morning. To say he wants your head served to him on a platter would be understating the case. He wants your balls cutting off with a rusty knife. He wants you roasted over an extremely slow spit. He wants—"

"I think I'm gettin' the picture," Woodend interrupted. "Anyroad, he's been on at me to get them four Poles locked up, an' that's just what I'm about to arrange now."

"So they did kill Gerhard Schultz?"

Woodend shook his head firmly. "No, they had absolutely nothin' to do with that."

"Then what *did* they do?"

Woodend told Chatterton what he'd found down by the lake. "That's how I know the Poles didn't kill Schultz," he said, when he'd finished.

Chatterton frowned. "Sorry if I'm being

thick, sir, but I'm afraid I don't quite follow your reasoning on that one."

"If they'd killed him, they'd never have done it in the woods, because the last thing they wanted was a load of bobbies swarmin' all over the area – bobbies who might have found out just what's been goin' on at the pumpin' station." His face adopted an unusually stern expression. "An' you should have found out, you know, Tim."

Chatterton bent his head slightly. "We didn't think to extend our search so far beyond the scene of the crime. But you're right, sir – it was incredibly sloppy work."

"Well, that's all behind us now," Woodend said, with characteristic generosity. "What have you been able to find out for me about Simon Hailsham and Mike Part-ridge?"

"What I've turned up on old Simon is pretty much what I expected to turn up. He's a Mason, as you know, and a member of the Rotary Club. He lives pretty much as you would imagine a man in his position would live – he's got a nice detached house in a good area, he goes to his local church nearly every Sunday, and plays a round of golf straight after it. I've got a lot more stuff along the same lines, but I don't suppose you'd be interested."

"No," Woodend agreed. "I wouldn't."

"Mike Partridge, on the other hand, has turned out to be something of a surprise."

"In what way?"

"Well, it turns out he does voluntary work at an old people's home in Maltham twice a week, but when I went down there and asked the matron about it, she was very cagey."

"Strange," Woodend said.

"I got the same response from the nurses at the hospital where he does some unpaid portering. As you can imagine, I was getting a bit suspicious by this point. Then I talked to my sergeant. He's a scoutmaster, and so is Partridge. Seems that a couple of years ago, the local paper was going to run a piece on all Partridge's good works. It was supposed to be a surprise, but he found out about it himself and he was furious."

"Was he now?"

"He told my sergeant he didn't want any sort of recognition for his good deeds. He said that would defeat the object of doing them in the first place."

"Interesting," Woodend said thoughtfully. "I think I'll have a word with Mr Partridge, when I can get round to it."

"To get back to the other thing," Chatterton said. "Now that you've got all the evidence you need, when do you plan to arrest the Poles?"

"I'm not goin' to arrest them." Woodend said.

"You're not?"

"It isn't my job. Besides, as desperately as they want to shift the stuff to somewhere safer, they'll not make a move as long as they think I might catch them at it. So I'm goin' to make myself as conspicuous as possible by stayin' in the bar all night—" he grinned – "which, as you know, will be a real hardship. An' in the meantime, your men can be hidin' in the woods, waitin' for them to turn up."

"I hope you don't think that arresting the Poles is going to make your problems with Mr Blake go away, sir," Chatterton cautioned him.

Woodend sighed. "No, I don't. If anythin', it'll make them worse, because it'll prove I was right about the Poles all along, an' leave Blake an' Hailsham lookin' like the pair of idiots we both know they are. But at least it'll stop Sexton from badgerin' me to arrest the wrong men for murder."

Twelve

It was six thirty in the evening by the time Bob Rutter's train pulled into Charing Cross station, and though he had been working since early morning and it was tempting to go straight home to his wife, he knew he could do no such thing until he had made at least two more calls. He hailed a taxi, and asked to be taken to 36 Hadfield Avenue, which, according to the personnel manager in BCI's Hereford plant, had been Gerhard Schultz's last address in London.

As the taxi sped along, Rutter tried to put his thoughts in order. He had learned a great deal about Mike Partridge, and even more about Simon Hailsham, but he had failed completely to find any link between either of those two men and Gerhard Schultz. And perhaps the reason he'd failed to find one was because there wasn't one to find. Perhaps if Schultz's death was linked in some way to his past, it was a different part of his past from the one the sergeant had spent the day investigating.

The taxi pulled up in front of a four-storey Victorian terraced house which had seen better days. Rutter paid off the cabby and walked up the path. There were a number of bells by the front door, and he pressed one of the two which belonged to the ground-floor flats. There was the sound of footsteps in the hallway, then the door was opened by a spotty youth with buck teeth and darting eyes, who was wearing striped pyjama bottoms and a vest.

"Yeah?" he said suspiciously.

"Police," Rutter said, producing his warrant card.

"But I haven't done nuffink," the youth said. "At least, nuffink I ain't already got caught for."

"Relax," Rutter said. "I'm not here to see you. You're too young to help me. I want to talk to somebody who was living here 1946."

The boy thought about it. "Old Man Thompson on the second floor's lived here for a long time," he said.

"Do you happen to know if he's at home?"

"Yeah, should be. Normally gets in from work at about half-past five." The youth paused. "I really haven't done nuffink, you know. I can show you a proper bill for that record player."

"But the television set's a bit dicey, isn't it?" Rutter said, taking a shot in the dark.

The boy looked shocked. "I'm only looking after that for a friend," he protested.

"Now how did I know you were going to say that?" Rutter mused. "Second floor, you said?"

"Yeah."

As Rutter climbed the stairs, he heard the young man scurrying back to his warren. He smiled to himself. He was not a betting man, but he would have been prepared to wager that by the time he came downstairs again, the dodgy television would be at least three streets away.

He stopped suddenly, as the realisation hit him that he would never have had anything like the same conversation with the spotty youth a couple of years earlier. Back then, he would have been much stiffer and more formal. Working with Woodend had certainly changed him. Christ, he was even starting to *sound* like Cloggin'-it Charlie. He sighed loudly – another Woodendian thing to do – and carried on climbing the stairs.

He knocked on the door on the second-floor landing. A man opened it. "Mr Thompson?" he asked.

"That's me."

'Old Man' Thompson was all of forty. He was of slight build, and had wispy blond hair which almost touched the collar of the bright-green silk dressing gown he wore over his shirt and trousers. His eyes were a faded blue, and there was wariness about them even before Rutter reached into his jacket pocket and produced his warrant card.

"I suppose you'd better come in," Thompson said resignedly.

"At times like this, most people normally say something like, 'What's this all about, Officer?'"

"Why should I bother saying that?" Thompson replied. "I know what it's all about. You want to ask me about Gerhard."

The living room into which Rutter followed the other man had a pleasant, comfortable feel about it – and certainly didn't seem to belong in a dilapidated terraced house. The carpet was a deep rich mustard colour, the curtains were heavy, and looked as if they might be velvet. The canary was chirping in its cage, and the goldfish was swimming in endless circles around its glass home; both blending in well with the general colour scheme. In the fireplace was one of those new-fangled electric fires with artificial coal and glowing, light-bulb-powered embers.

"Would you care for a cup of tea?" Thompson asked. "I've just brewed it. It's a special China blend they make up for me in a shop in Knightsbridge. It's rather delicate."

"A cup of tea would be very nice," Rutter told him.

Thompson walked over to his kitchenette, and poured the tea into fine bone-china cups. "Would you like a slice of lemon with it?" he asked. "Or are you one of those people who insist on taking it with milk?"

"I think I would rather prefer milk."

Thompson tut-tutted. "It ruins the flavour, you know, but I suppose it's a case of *chacun à son goût.*" He crossed the room and handed Rutter a cup. "Well, sit down, dear boy. One can't possibly savour a good cup of tea – even tea with milk in it – when one is standing up."

Rutter sat, and so did Thompson.

"Yes," the man in the dressing gown continued, more serious now, "I've been expecting a visit from the police ever since I read about Gerhard's death in the news-papers."

"Did you know him well?"

"Very well. At least for a while."

"When did you meet him?"

"When he first moved into the house. That would have been sometime in 1946, just

206

after he was released from the prisoner-of-war camp."

"And you soon became friends?"

"That's right."

"Do you know, I've talked to a number of people about him," Rutter said. "but you're the first one who'll admit to having been his friend. Now why do you think that is?"

"I can't speak for his other relationships, only about the one I had with him. We knew we were going to get along with each other right from the start. It's hard to explain exactly how we knew, but it was as if there was some kind of spark between us."

"What sort of thing did you do together?"

"Oh, nothing out of the ordinary. Sometimes I'd cook him a good square meal – he couldn't so much as boil an egg himself, poor lamb – and sometimes we'd share a bottle of inexpensive wine. And talk! We seemed to talk about everything under the sun."

"Why did he come to London?" Rutter asked, taking out his packet of cork-tipped cigarettes.

"I'd rather you didn't smoke, if you don't mind," Thompson said. "The smell does tend to cling to the soft furnishings and it makes me feel quite nauseous. Now what was your question again?"

"Why did he come to London?" Rutter

repeated, slipping the cigarettes regretfully back in his pocket.

"He was looking for work. He thought there'd be more opportunities in the big city."

"And were there?"

Thompson shook his head. "Not the right sort of work, anyway. He'd been an officer, a war hero – he had the Iron Cross, you know – and he found himself working behind a bar. But I will say this for him – he wasn't bitter. He said there was dignity in any kind of honest labour."

"How long did he work in the pub?"

"Not long. He had a stroke of good luck. Or, at least, that's what I used to believe."

"And what do you think now?"

"Now I think that men like Gerhard – men of action – make their own luck. Anyway, he met a man in the pub where he was working..."

"The personnel manager from BCI Hereford."

"That's right. And he was offered a job on the spot. He was very excited about it. He carried the letter the man sent him around in his wallet, almost as if it were a love letter, and now and again he'd take it out and read it. Not that it was anything special – it just said it had been a pleasure to meet him in the pub and put the job offer in writing. But it was his big chance, you see. For all he talked about the dignity of all labour, I think there was a small part of him which did find it humiliating to work in a bar."

"You must have been happy for him yourself," Rutter said.

"Not really. I was a bit depressed about the thought of him going away, if the truth be told. But Gerhard said there was no need for the blues, because it wasn't as if Hereford was the other side of the world, and we'd still see each other most weekends."

"And did you?"

"I'll get to that in a minute," Thompson said. "About a week before he was due to leave for Hereford, he got a letter from Germany, and after he'd read it, he told me he had to go away for a couple of days on business."

"To Germany?"

"No."

"Then where?"

"He said the business was in Liverpool. Anyway, that was the last I ever saw of him."

"He didn't come back?"

"Oh, he came back all right," Thompson said, a bitter edge creeping into his tone. "He came back in the middle of the night. Like a thief. He didn't have that many belongings – it was a furnished flat he was living in – but what he did have, he packed up. He wasn't supposed to vacate the flat for another week or so, but he left the landlord a whole month's rent in lieu of notice." He paused to sip his tea, and Rutter noticed the moisture in his eyes. "He didn't leave anything for me though," he continued, "not even a note."

"Didn't you write to him?" Rutter asked. "After all, it would have been easy enough for you to find out the address of the BCI factory in Hereford."

Thompson sighed. "No, I didn't write to him."

"Why not?"

"What would have been the point? Leaving the way he did, he was as good as saying our friendship was over."

"You felt betrayed?" Rutter suggested.

"Yes, I suppose that is one way of putting it. But it was all a long time ago – I'm over it now."

Are you? Rutter wondered. Are you really?

Rutter's luck seemed to be in. The pub where Gerhard Schultz had worked briefly was called the Eagle and Child, and the landlord, Wally Stubbs, had been there ever since the end of 1945. He was lucky, too, to have arrived at a quiet time, so that Stubbs was more than willing to talk to him.

"So you were the person who gave Schultz

a job in the first place?" the detective said.

"That's right," Stubbs agreed.

"Didn't it bother you, employing a German flier so soon after the end of the war?"

"Might have done if he'd been one of the ones who'd flown a bomber," Stubbs admitted. "The Blitz were still very much in people's memories at that time. Well, they'd only to look around them and see all the bombsites to be reminded. But a fighter pilot was a different matter. There was a bit of glamour about him. Even a lot of the people who were rabid anti-Germans had a grudging admiration for blokes like Gerhard."

"So he got on well with your customers?"

"There were a few miserable old sods who muttered into their beer about me hiring a Kraut, but it didn't bother most of the regulars. Gerhard was a very good barman, you see. You only had to order a drink from him the once, and the next time you came into the pub it'd be waiting on the counter for you. He always had a pleasant manner about him, and if you had a bit of misery you wanted to spill out, he made a good listener."

A man in a flat cap, with a greyhound on a lead, walked up to the bar. "No danger of gettin' a drink, is there, Wally?" he asked.

The landlord grinned at him. "Be right with you, Stan." He turned to Rutter. "If you'll excuse me for a minute."

Left alone, Rutter sifted the information he had collected so far. From what the landlord had said, it sounded like Schultz had been a nice man but becoming a manager at BCI had changed all that. The sympathetic barman who remembered what everybody drank had turned into the ruthless efficiency expert who could talk with relish about cutting other people's jobs. The sergeant supposed it was just the way things were in this life. Those stern, humourless commanders back at the Yard must once – surely – have been eager fresh-faced young constables, patting little kids on the head and helping old ladies across the street.

Having served a pint to the man with the greyhound, Wally Stubbs returned to his former position opposite Rutter. "What else would you like to know about Gerhard?" he asked.

"Did he ever tell you anything about his personal life?"

"Not really."

"Not even a hint?"

The landlord scratched his head. "Well, there was that one time, when I was telling him about this friend of mine."

"Carry on," Rutter said encouragingly.

"Jackie Philips, his name was. We'd been in the North African campaign together. Right through from the beginning to the end. Well, he was living in Leeds at the time, but he wanted to come down to London so he wrote to me and asked if I could put him up for a couple of nights. Of course, I was delighted, and wrote back at once to say yes."

"Excuse me, sir, but what's any of this got to do with Gerhard Schultz?" Rutter interrupted.

"Sorry, I do go on a bit, don't I?" Stubbs said, apologetically. "The point is, I was telling Gerhard about Jackie's letter, and he said, 'I once had a good friend, too.' That was all. But the way he said it, it aroused my curiosity, you see. So I said, 'What happened to him? Was he killed in the war?' And he said, 'It would have been far better for him if he had been.' Then he wandered off to the other end of the bar and started polishing glasses."

"And that was it?"

"Not quite. He was very moody for the rest of the night, not himself at all. Then, just as he was leaving, about half an hour after closing time, he came up to the bar. 'Do you mind if I ask you a question, Wally?' he asked. I said, of course I didn't. Then his eyes came over all strange, almost as if he was going into a trance. 'Do you think that we have a sacred duty to our friends?' he asked, and he was speaking so softly it was almost a whisper. 'Do you think we have the right to seek out justice for them, even if it means breaking man's laws – even if it means breaking *God's* laws?'"

"What did you tell him?"

"Well, at first I was so taken aback that I couldn't think of what to say to him. But finally I came up with something like, that kind of question was a bit deep for me, especially so late at night. But I don't think he was listening, anyway. He wasn't so much talking to me, you see, as talking it through with himself. But what he said must have had some impact mustn't it, or I wouldn't still remember it after all these years?"

"Did you ever try to talk to Schultz about the subject again?" Bob Rutter asked.

The landlord shook his head. "Never really got the chance. A couple of days later, he handed in his notice. Seemed he'd been offered a better job – in a big chemical factory somewhere."

"You've been a great help, Mr Stubbs," Rutter said, but he was thinking that, like so many great helps, the pub landlord had raised more questions than he'd answered.

It was good to have her Bob arrive home unexpectedly, Maria Rutter thought, but at the same time she had to be very careful not to show how much of a relief it was as well. It was the pregnancy which was the real problem. She'd learned how to cope quite well with being blind, but having the responsibility for another, tiny human life on top of that felt such a burden that she was sure it was about to crush her.

"You'll manage, Maria," she told herself fiercely. "You'll *have to* manage – because there's no other choice."

She turned her head in the direction of the hallway, and wondered how much longer Bob would be on the phone to Charlie Woodend.

Woodend stood at the bar of the Westbury Social Club, a pint in one hand, the phone in the other, and a Capstan Full Strength hanging from the corner of his mouth. As he listened to Rutter's report on Mike Partridge, Simon Hailsham and Gerhard Schultz, he was aware that the sole occupant of the Polish table was watching him with a mixture of suspicion and hostility. And why weren't the rest of Poles there? Because they'd be getting their tools together, ready to slip into the woods and do a bit of dismantling.

"I think this letter that Schultz received from Germany, just before he moved to Hereford, could be very significant," Rutter was saying.

"So do I," Woodend agreed. "In fact, even without the letter, I'd already made the decision that we'd never get to the bottom of this without takin' the German end of things firmly by the horns. I was on the phone earlier this evenin', gettin' the authorisation from the commander."

"Authorisation for what?" Rutter asked, and Woodend thought he could detect a note of concern creeping into his sergeant's voice – as if he already suspected what was coming, and didn't like it one bit.

"The authorisation for you to fly to Bavaria an' interview Schultz's family and friends," the chief inspector said.

"Couldn't the German police do that?"

"I suppose they *could* do the job..." the chief inspector admitted.

"Well, then..."

"But I'd be much happier with you on the scene. An' take my word for it, you'd not be much use up here. The trail's gone so cold that all I can do is wait for a lucky break."

"Why don't you go to Germany, and I'll handle things in Cheshire?" Rutter suggested.

"Because I'm already on the scene,"

Woodend reminded him. "Besides, I've done my share of chasing Krauts around Germany. An' anyway, the ticket's already booked in your name. You take off at ten thirty tomorrow mornin'. You have to check in about an hour an' a half earlier. Make sure you're on time. They probably had to bump some other poor bugger off the flight to make room for you, so they're not goin' to be too pleased if you miss it."

"I won't miss it," Rutter promised.

"Then I'll see you when you get back," Woodend said. "Good luck, an' watch yourself on that strong German ale – it can creep up on you better than any Panzer Division."

He handed the phone back to Tony the bar steward, and turned to face the Polish table again. Still just one man – still watching him.

You'd do better to worry about what's goin' on in the woods right now, lad, he thought as he ordered himself another pint.

Maria could tell from his heavy footsteps as he walked down the hall that something was wrong with Bob, and wondered what nice Charlie Woodend could have possibly said to make him so depressed.

She did not have to wait long to find out. "Cloggin'-it Charlie wants me to clog it

217

around the Federal Republic of Germany," Rutter said.

"Well, that's good, isn't?"

"Good?"

"Sending you off to Germany on your own just shows how much confidence he has in you."

"I know, but..."

"But what?"

Rutter knelt down by his wife's chair, and took her hands in his. "It'll mean flying," he said.

"But of course it will."

"I've never flown before – and even the thought of it terrifies me."

Maria laughed. "Why should you be worried? Flying is – what do you call it? – a piece of cake."

"That's easy for you to say," Rutter countered. "You've been flying since you were a baby."

Maria broke free of his grip, and began to stroke his hair. "It will be all right," she cooed. "I'll come with you to the airport."

"But how will you get back?"

"By taxi, of course."

"But you're..."

"I'm blind," Marie said. "And I'm going to have a baby. If I can't manage a taxi on my own, then we really are in trouble."

It was nearly closing time in the Westbury Social Club, but the Polish watcher was still at his post.

What would he do if I got up now an' headed for the woods? the chief inspector wondered. Attack me, like he or one of his mates did last night? Or try an' get ahead of me to warn the others?

It didn't really matter either way, because, as he'd made clear to Inspector Chatterton, he had no intention of doing the local bobbies' job for them.

It had been foolish of Rozpedek to offer him a drink of vodka from an unlabelled bottle, but no more foolish than it had been for the Polish cavalry to charge German tanks. Just being Polish seemed to carry with it an element of bravado. But that bravado would have to be paid for. Customs and Excise took a dim view of men who distilled spirits in their spare time, and the four Poles would be lucky to get away without a gaol sentence.

The chief inspector contemplated setting off up the lane in search of the Dark Lady, but as Luigi Bernadelli was sitting at his customary table, he didn't think she would be appearing that particular night. Perhaps, instead, he would go to bed with a good book.

He thought of the volumes in the dead

man's room – books which had been bought for show, rather than pleasure. *A Tale of Two Cities* had been there. He wondered why it had always been one of his favourite Dickens novels. Possibly it was because of the central character, Sidney Carton, who so resembles Charles Darney that he can take his place at the guillotine. And why is he willing to sacrifice his own life? He does it for two reasons. The first is that he loves Darney's wife, Lucie, and cannot bear the thought of the unhappiness that the news of Darney's death will bring down on her. The second is that he considers his own life to be so worthless that he hopes to give it meaning by this one selfless act.

But could the act be truly selfless if he was hoping to get something out of it? Woodend asked himself, as he drained the last inch of his pint. Mike Partridge didn't think so – he'd said as much to Chatterton's sergeant, who was a fellow scoutmaster – but the chief inspector wasn't entirely convinced he was right. Maybe rereading Dickens would give him the answer. Or perhaps it would teach him that there were no answers. That was what was so good about the Great Man – he made you think until your brain hurt.

Tony called last orders and Woodend asked for a bottle of whisky to take up to his room.

As he made his way up the stairs, he reached into the pocket of his hairy sports jacket and took out the key to Gerhard Schultz's room. The German had even less use for *A Tale of Two Cities* now he was dead than he had when he was alive. No harm could come from borrowing it, just as no harm had come from Rutter borrowing *The Pickwick Papers* – not that Woodend was convinced the young bugger would ever read it.

He unlocked Schultz's door and stepped into the room. He made a move to turn on the light, then stopped himself. He stood perfectly still in the darkness, trying to absorb the atmosphere of the place.

At first, he felt nothing, just as he had done the last time he visited the room. It was almost as if the German who had lived there for almost two months had had no personality of his own – or else had kept it locked up so tightly that it was as pale as a prisoner serving a lifetime in solitary confinement.

And then, he did start to sense something. It began as the vaguest hint of a feeling, but as he waited in the darkness, it grew and grew, until it was filling the whole room and all but choking him. He could taste it in his throat, he could feel it coiling around his body. He did not know exactly what it was he had released, but he knew that it was horribly – darkly – evil.

Woodend staggered over to the wall and hit the switch. Instantly, the room was bathed in light, and equally instantly whatever ghastly apparition he had been sharing it with was gone.

The chief inspector took a deep breath. Could this be the room in which Lady Caroline Sutton had murdered her husband? Would that be enough to account for the horrendous sensation which had lasted only a few seconds, but which had shaken him to his very core?

Woodend walked over to the bookshelf and extracted *A Tale of Two Cities*. A couple of stiff Scotches and a couple of meaty chapters of Dickens should be enough to put the experience behind him, he thought. Then he would be ready for a good night's sleep.

Back in his own room, he undressed, put on the flannel pyjamas which his wife had so carefully ironed before packing, poured the first of the two Scotches he had promised himself, and climbed into bed.

"It was the best of times, it was the worst of times," he read, "it was the age of wisdom, it was the age of foolishness, it was the epoch of belief, it was the epoch of incredulity, it was the season of Light, it was the season of Darkness, it was the spring of hope, it was the winter of despair..."

Without taking his eyes off the page, Woodend took a sip of his drink. Bloody marvellous writin', he thought.

He turned the page, and something fell out of the book. It was a single sheet of paper, roughly torn from a cheap writing block. It was probably nothing of importance, he told himself, but it should have been spotted by the local flatfeet when they searched the room, and it obviously hadn't been.

He placed his drink on the bedside table, and put his book down on the counterpane next to him. It was his training, rather than any anticipation, which made him pick up the sheet carefully by the corner. And then he saw what was written on it.

"Bloody hell fire!" he said to his empty room.

The message was written in red ink, and was in large block capital letters:

THINK OF THE DARK LADY
DO YOU FEEL NO SHAME?

How long had the message been in the book? Woodend asked himself. Had Schultz received it while he was still working in Hereford, or had it been sent to him in Cheshire?

Come to that, how did he know it had been sent to Schultz at all? Wasn't it possible that Schultz had written it himself, and had been intending to send it to someone else when he was killed?

Putting the letter carefully on the cabinet, Woodend picked up his whisky glass, and took a small sip.

What the bloody hell did it mean? *Think of the Dark Lady. Have you no shame?*

Could it possibly be Lady Caroline Sutton the writer was referring to, or was there, as he already suspected, another Dark Lady in Gerhard Schultz's past?

Woodend was surprised to see that he had drunk all his whisky. He unscrewed the cap on the bottle, and poured himself another shot. A few minutes earlier he had been anticipating a good night's sleep, but he knew himself well enough to accept that now he had seen the note he would get very little rest.

Thirteen

It was as if the benevolent sunshine and clear blue skies under which Woodend had met Gretchen Müller the previous day had never existed. In their place hung heavy black clouds, glowering with disdain on Westbury Park. The change in the weather seemed to affect everyone and everything. People walked with less of a spring in their steps. Cats showed none of their usual alertness. Birds chirped in a mechanical way, as if they were only going through the motions. And the brightly painted houses of the park looked as dull and insubstantial as the converted army huts they secretly were.

The weather even seemed to have affected Tony, the normally cheerful bar steward, who could barely raise a smile when he brought in Woodend's fried breakfast and daily newspapers. The chief inspector picked up the *Daily Mirror* first. There was no mention of the Dark Lady of Westbury

Hall on the front page, but he suspected that the story still had too much mileage in it to have been dropped completely. He was right. On page seven, next to the photograph of a man who used cigarettes as the filling for his sandwiches, was a short piece by Elizabeth Driver.

Death and the Dark Lady

The Dark Lady of Westbury Hall in quiet rural Cheshire was reported to have been sighted again last night. Legend has it that the supposed ghost of Lady Caroline Sutton only appears when a death is imminent. While some of the local people believe the story to be merely fanciful, there are others who point out that it was after her first appearance that Gerhard Schultz, a British Chemical Industries executive, was found brutally murdered in the woods near Westbury Hall, and the question on many lips is this – Is the Dark Lady's appearance no more than a reminder that there has already been one killing, or is it a foreshadowing of more deaths to come?

The girl did have spirit, but Bob Rutter, for all his middle-aged attitude, was quite right. Elizabeth Driver's stories were making the people at BCI nervous, and that had already had an impact on the investigation – so those stories were going to have to stop.

The door to the breakfast room swung open, and Inspector Chatterton walked in.

"Well, we caught the Poles," he said, without any hint of satisfaction in his voice. "It was just like you told us it was going to be. They had their tools with them, and they were going to dismantle the still and move it somewhere safer."

"But ... ?" Woodend asked.

"But just as you suspected yesterday, it hasn't made the chief constable any happier. He's been going round the station muttering that he's been on to the Yard again, and he's been told on good authority that your days here are very much numbered."

Woodend nodded. "I'm goin' to have to give him Fred Foley. It won't do him any good, because the man's innocent an' you'll never be able prove otherwise – but at least it'll buy me some time."

"You know where Fred Foley is?" Chatterton asked incredulously.

"Yes, I do."

"But how could you? We've had men out searching for days, and we still haven't found him, yet you've never left the park."

"I have a trick I use," Woodend said. "An' it's this: when people tell me things, I listen."

As Bob Rutter's taxi approached the turning for London Airport, snippets of disturbing information which he wasn't even aware that he knew kept popping into his mind:

Five members of the crew and two passengers had been killed when a British European Airways Viscount crashed on the approach to Nott's Corner Airport in Belfast.

Another Viscount had collided with an Italian fighter plane near Anzio, and crashed with the loss of all thirty-one people on board.

Maria's hand gently squeezed his lower arm. "You feel so tense," she said. "There's really no need for it, you know."

"I do know," Rutter replied unconvincingly.

But he was thinking, And then there's the famous one, the one that everybody remembers.

Just over three years earlier, a BEA Ambassador had failed to clear a fence when taking off from Rhiem airport. The plane had been carrying the Manchester United team, who were celebrating qualifying for a place in the semi-finals of the European Cup.

Rutter had seen the pictures in the newspapers. The plane had been no more than a shattered shell – a twisted, distorted wreck. Eight members of the team had been killed, along with thirteen other passengers.

"You're still thinking about planes crashing, aren't you, my darling?" Maria asked.

"It's hard not to when there seems to have been so many of them," Rutter admitted.

"Not so many at all," Maria assured him. "Certainly not in comparison to the number of flights. I got the operator to ring BEA for me. Do you know that they carried over half a million passengers last year? Everybody's travelling by plane these days. There's even a regular service to America now."

Rutter lit one of his corked-tipped cigarettes. Maria's assurances were all very well, he told himself, but what did they call the crash which killed all those Manchester United players? The Munich Air Disaster. And where was he flying to? Bloody Munich!

"Listen, the Comet's a very big plane," Maria persisted. "It's got a crew of four, and it carries over sixty passengers. It's safer than a bus."

"Buses don't hang up in the sky with no visible means of support," Rutter said gloomily.

Maria squeezed his arm again. "I love you

so much that I'd *know* if anything was going to go wrong," she whispered softly. "I'd know – and I wouldn't let you fly."

It was a silly thing to say, Rutter thought. Love had nothing to do with seeing into the future. In all the cases he'd investigated, the death of a loved one had always come as a complete shock to the victim's friends and family. And yet, even knowing that, he found that after Maria's soothing words he was suddenly starting to feel a little better.

Mike Partridge lived in a modern block of flats on the edge of Maltham. The place was probably owned by BCI, just as everything else in the town seemed to be, Woodend thought grumpily as he climbed the stairs to the second floor.

He rang Partridge's bell. He heard the sound of movement from the other side of the door, but after perhaps half a minute had passed, it became obvious that no one was going to open it for him.

He rang again. And then a third time. Still he was ignored, and it was only by resorting to the tactic of keeping his finger permanently on the bell that he finally brought Partridge to the door.

"What the bloody 'ell do you want?" the red-faced shift man demanded gruffly.

"I've got a few questions I'd rather like

answers to," the chief inspector replied.

"I've answered all your questions once," Partridge countered. "That should be enough for you."

"Maybe it would have been if you'd told me the complete truth," Woodend said. "But you didn't, did you?"

"I don't know what you're talkin' about."

"The last time we spoke, you did everythin' you could to create the impression that you were a bachelor. But you're not. You're a widower."

Partridge's eyes flashed with anger. "You've been checkin' up on me," he said accusingly.

"Well, of course I have. That's my job. Did you really expect me to do anythin' else?"

The shift man sighed. "I suppose not."

"I don't like talkin' to people in corridors," Woodend said. "They're nasty, draughty places. I'd much rather be inside."

"Why should I let you into my flat?"

"Why shouldn't you let me in? Unless, of course, you've got somethin' to hide?"

Partridge shrugged, then turned around and re-entered his flat. Woodend followed him down the short hallway and into his living room. It was a sparse, soulless place. There were no pictures on the walls, and no ornaments on the mantelpiece or sideboard. The only personal touch of any kind was a framed photograph on the windowsill. Here was a man who used his flat as nothing more than a place to sleep.

Woodend walked over to the window to take a closer look at the photograph. It was of a young woman, who was proudly holding an apple-cheeked child in her arms.

"When was this taken?" he asked.

"1940," Partridge replied dully. "The kiddie would 'ave been twenty-three if she'd lived. She might even 'ave been married. I could 'ave been a grandfather by now."

"A lot of the children in Southampton were evacuated to the countryside, but your family stayed with you," Woodend said. "Why was that? Wasn't there anywhere you could send her?"

"Oh yes, there was somewhere I could 'ave sent her. My wife 'ad a sister who lived in the country. She invited Doris an' the kiddie to go an' live with 'er, but Doris decided to stay with me."

"Tell me about your girlfriend – the Dark Lady."

If the chief inspector had been expecting Partridge's ruddy face to go suddenly pale, he would have been disappointed, because the expression which filled it at that moment was far more complex than simple guilt.

"She was Jamaican," he said. "I'd seen a

232

few coloured merchant seamen down at the docks, but I'd never met a black *woman* before. I loved my wife, but this was different. Lucinda was so ... so..." He waved his hands, frustrated at his lack of ability to express himself. "She didn't think things through. She just did what she wanted to do. She was ... what's the word?"

"Spontaneous?" Woodend supplied.

"That's it. Spontaneous. She loved life, an' was determined to squeeze the last drop out of it. I fell for 'er in a big way. I wanted 'er, but at the same time I wanted my family." He laughed bitterly. "That was 'ow I was in those days. Always wantin' to 'ave my cake an' eat it too."

"After your family was killed, did you think of settin' up house with your Dark Lady?" Woodend asked.

Partridge shook his head. "She wanted to, but I couldn't. I ... just ... couldn't."

"So you joined the army instead," Woodend said. "You didn't have to – the job you were doin' was considered vital war work, so you'd never have been called up – but you wanted to go into battle, didn't you?"

"No, I wanted to die," Partridge corrected him. "I *expected* to die. But all I got was a bullet in the leg." He paused, as if a thought had suddenly struck him. "I can see where this is leadin' now," he said, anger entering his voice again. "My wife an' little daughter were killed by a German bomb, an' when a German flier came to Westbury Park, I just couldn't bear it. So I killed 'im. Isn't that what you're about to tell me?"

Woodend shook his head. "I might have thought that, but for what you said to Horace Greenwood."

"Horace?" Partridge repeated. "You talked to him?"

"No, my sergeant was the one who saw him. But that's neither here nor there, is it? It's what he told us that's important. He visited you in hospital after the D-Day landin'."

"I remember that."

"An' all you would say to him was, 'It's my fault. It's all my fault.' He thought you were talkin' about the men who'd died durin' the invasion – men you'd promised would come through it all in one piece. But I don't think you were meanin' that at all. Am I right?"

Partridge bowed his head. "Yes, you're right," he agreed. "I lied earlier, when I told you that my wife 'ad decided not to go an' stay with her sister in the country. She wanted to go, an' I talked 'er out of it because what *I* wanted was to have 'er an' the baby there when I came home from work. It wasn't the Germans who killed her

234

– it was me. I killed them both."

"An' ever since then, you've been tryin' to atone for it," Woodend said sadly. "You've not looked at another woman since your wife died. You do a lot of charity work, but you don't claim any credit for it. An' you can't see anybody in trouble without wantin' to help them, can you?"

"No," Partridge admitted. "I can't."

"The night Gerhard Schultz was killed? You didn't come straight home, did you?"

"Why would I?" Partridge asked, making a sweeping gesture with his hand. "What is there 'ere to come 'ome to?"

"So what did you do instead?"

"I'm not really sure. I suppose I must have just walked around the park, thinkin'."

From beyond the bedroom door came the muffled sound of a dog barking.

"I wouldn't have put you down as the sort of feller to keep a pet, Mr Partridge," Woodend said.

"It was a stray, wanderin' the streets. A poor, 'alf-starved thing. I was sorry for it."

Woodend shook his head disbelievingly. "I've never known a man who kept a dog say he had nothin' to come home to. An' I've never known a man who had a dog who wouldn't introduce it to his visitors." He took his Capstan Full Strength out of his pocket, and lit one up. "Come on, Mr

Partridge! Isn't it time we stopped playin' games an' brought Fred Foley out here?"

"You want me to 'elp you with that, darlin'?" the taxi driver asked, as Maria ran her fingers over the coins in her purse.

"No, thank you," she answered. "I can manage quite well on my own."

"I wouldn't steal from yer, or anyfink like that!" the cabbie said, sounding slightly offended.

"I'm sure you wouldn't," Maria told him. "It's just that the more things I learn to do on my own, the easier it is."

She handed over the fare, opened the gate, and, using her white stick, tapped her way carefully up the path. She still found it incredible that Bob – her big, strong husband – had been so afraid of a simple thing like flying. But then, she supposed, fear was rarely very rational. There were people who were afraid of being in enclosed spaces, and people who were afraid of wide-open spaces. Some were frightened of heights, others of dogs.

And some people were afraid to ask for things because it might draw attention to the fact that they were blind.

She slotted her key into the front door – it was getting easier every time she did it – and stepped into the hallway. She could hear the sound of vigorous vacuuming from the living room. That German girl would wear the Hoover out, she thought with a smile.

"Ah, you are home, Mrs Rutter," the au pair shouted over the noise of the machine.

"Switch that off, please, Ute," Maria said. "There's something I want to ask you."

The vacuum cleaner fell silent.

"Yes, madam?"

"Ever since you got here, I've been wondering what you look like. How would you describe yourself?"

There was a pause, then Ute said in an embarrassed voice, "I am quite ordinary. Quite normal."

"Could I touch your face?" Maria asked. "Just so I get an impression of your features?"

"Of course."

Of course! Was that what she'd actually said?

"You really don't mind?" Maria asked, hardly able to believe it.

"I haf a grandmother who is blind," Ute said. "Always she touches my face ven I go to see her."

"Stand closer to me," Maria said, and when Ute had done so, she lifted her hands.

The German girl was taller than she'd thought. As her fingers explored, she was building up a picture in her mind. Slightly

237

upturned nose, wide mouth, and rounded chin. It was a pleasant face, and knowing about it made her feel as if she'd got to know the au pair a little better, too.

"Thank you, Ute," she said.

"It vas nothing," the German girl said.

But it was! It really was! And it was a wonderful thing to be pregnant! There were going to be difficult times ahead, but she was sure now that she could get through them.

The man standing just beyond the barrier at Rhiem Airport was not very tall for a policeman, but had enormous square shoulders. His hair was blond and clipped very short. Despite the heat, he was wearing a black leather jacket, and he was smoking an HB cigarette with all the intensity of someone who took everything he did seriously. When he saw Rutter, he stepped forward and held out his hand.

"Inspector Hans Kohl," he announced, pumping the English detective's hand vigorously. "Welcome to Germany, Sergeant Rutter. I am to be your guide for as long as you are here, and – when necessary – your interpreter."

Rutter, who had decided after getting off the flight unscathed that he finally knew what the survivors of the *Titanic* must have felt like, pumped the German's hand back.

"I don't know how well you've been briefed, but the reason I'm here is to find out all I can about a man called Gerhard Schultz..." he began

"Ja, ja, that has all been arranged," Inspector Kohl said brusquely. "I have a car waiting outside. It should not take much more than an hour to reach the town where his parents live. They have already been told to expect you."

He was standing on foreign soil, Rutter realised now he had put his fear of the flight behind him and had time to think. He was actually in another country. And he knew absolutely nothing about it. He didn't even know where he'd be spending the night.

"Have you fixed up any accommodation for me, sir?" Rutter asked, doing his best to sound like Woodend.

"But of course. I have booked both of us into a small hotel in Herr Schultz's home town. That means that if you wish to question the parents again tomorrow morning, we will be in walking distance of the house. And if you do not wish to see them, well, I'm told the hotel is a good place to stay, with excellent food and plentiful beer. I hope that is satisfactory."

"Very satisfactory," said Rutter, who was rapidly coming to the conclusion that whatever else happened while he was in the country, he was certainly going to enjoy working with the German police.

Fred Foley stood in Mike Partridge's bedroom doorway, his mangy dog by his side. The man had looked a real mess the last time Woodend had met him – during the Salton case – but he was even worse now. His eyes were so bloodshot it was almost impossible to detect any white. His nose was a mass of blackheads. His hands shook, and his jaw wobbled. And there was a distinct whiff about him.

"I try to get 'im to wash every day, but it's not always easy," Partridge said apologetically.

"What about booze?" Woodend asked.

"I'm slowly tryin' to wean him off it. 'E 'asn't had much today, but there must still be a hell of a lot floatin' around in 'is system."

Woodend turned his attention on Foley, who was still standing uncertainly in the doorway.

"Can you hear me, Mr Foley?" he asked. "Do you understand what I'm sayin'?"

The other man merely nodded.

"The reason you've been hangin' around Westbury Park so much for the past year or so was because of the Poles, wasn't it?" the chief inspector asked. "If you went down to the old pumpin' station by the lake when they were there, they'd sometimes give you some of that vodka they made. Am I right?"

Foley licked his dry lips. "Yes," he croaked.

"You were down there the night the German was killed. They gave you enough booze to get you well an' truly plastered, an' then you went wanderin' off into the woods."

"I don't remember much," Foley admitted.

"But you do remember findin' Schultz, don't you?"

"He was lyin' on the ground. I didn't see him. I tripped over his feet an' landed right on top of him."

"An' that's how you came to get his blood on your overcoat. What happened next?"

"I panicked," Foley said. "I'd already been involved in one murder case. I didn't want to get caught up in another. I got out of the woods as quick as I could, an' started headin' for Maltham. I didn't know what I was goin' to do when I got there. It ... it was just somewhere to go. Then I felt these pains in my belly, an' I had to stop to be sick."

"Which is when you met Mr Partridge?"

"He was cyclin' past. He stopped to see if

I was all right. I told him what had happened."

"'E swore to me that 'e 'adn't done the killin', an' I believed him," Partridge said.

"So the first thing you did was to throw his coat behind the nearest hedge, an' the second was to bring him here – which is where he an' his dog have been ever since."

"I didn't think 'e could face bein' questioned by the police, the state 'e was in."

"But you did know he'd have to face them eventually, didn't you, Mr Partridge?"

Partridge shrugged. "I suppose I did, but I 'adn't really thought that far ahead."

"I can't go the police," Fred Foley whimpered. "They'll lock me up an' never let me out again."

"They'll lock you up," Woodend conceded, "but not for long. Without a signed confession, there's nowhere near enough evidence to hold you for more than a couple of days. So you're goin' to have to be strong, Mr Foley. You're goin' to have to pull yourself together – at least for the time you're in custody. Do you think you can do that?"

"I'll try," Foley promised.

"Right, you an' me had better get ourselves down to the local nick," Woodend said.

"What about me?" Mike Partridge asked.

"What about you?" Woodend replied.

"I've been 'idin' a wanted man for days. Won't the bobbies want to arrest me, an' all?"

"You've only been doin' what you thought was right, an' placed in your situation, I'm not sure I'd have behaved any differently myself," Woodend said. He turned back to Foley. "What are you goin' to tell the police when they ask you where I found you?"

Foley looked down at the floor. "I don't know."

"Then why not simply tell them the truth," Woodend suggested, "which is that I found you wanderin' around in the woods behind Westbury Park."

"Yes," Foley agreed, nodding gravely. "That's exactly what I'll tell them."

Fourteen

Inspector Kohl kept the black Mercedes Benz at just under the speed limit as he drove through a series of villages so unbelievably neat and tidy that they might have been expecting a visit from royalty at any moment. Rutter, sitting next to him, had now got over the shock of still being alive, and was starting to enjoy 'abroad'.

"Do you know anything about the Schultz family's background?" the Englishman asked the German.

"But of course," Inspector Kohl replied, as if he were surprised that Rutter even needed to ask such a question. "The dead man's mother and father are both in their early seventies. Before they retired, they both taught English in ... how would you say it? – in gymnasiums."

"In secondary schools," Rutter corrected.

"Yes, you are right," Kohl agreed, and Rutter was sure the German would never make that same mistake over the word again.

"They have three children, two boys and girl, " Kohl continued. "Gerhard was the youngest. Herr Schultz, the father, was a captain in the First World War, and was awarded the Iron Cross, as his son also was in the Second World War. Since early middle age, Herr Schultz has suffered from gout. Both the parents regularly attend their local church – they are Catholics, as are most Bavarians – and Frau Schultz is an active member of its Ladies Committee. I am sorry that I do not have any more information for you, but you must understand that I was only given this assignment three hours ago."

Rutter whistled softly to himself – and wondered how the Germans had ever managed to lose the war.

They were entering a small town. The houses were all solid and detached. They had large windows, and almost impossibly steep slate roofs which were glistening in the warm afternoon sun. If the town had been damaged during the war, there was absolutely no indication of it now.

Kohl brought the Mercedes to a halt in front of one of the houses. "This is the place," he said.

They walked up the path. The front door

opened, and a man who had obviously been listening for their arrival stepped out to greet them.

If this was Herr Schultz, he looked considerably older than his seventy-odd years, Rutter thought. It wasn't just that his hair was white and his skin incredibly wrinkled. It wasn't even that he was leaning heavily on his carved walking stick. He carried with him the air of man who had experienced nothing but incredible suffering for at least a century.

The old man held out his hand to the English policeman. "I am Wolfgang Schultz," he said formally.

"Bob Rutter."

Herr Schultz twisted his aged body to shake hands with Inspector Kohl, then said, "Welcome to my home. Please follow me. My wife is waiting for us inside the house."

Like her husband, Mrs Schultz was small and white-haired – and also like him seemed shrouded in a mantle of grief. Shaking her thin, dry hand, Rutter found it hard to believe that these two fragile people had produced a baby which had turned into a strapping man called Gerhard Schultz.

"Please be seated, gentlemen," Herr Schultz said, indicating the sofa. "You will take some refreshment? A coffee? A little wine?"

Rutter shook his head. "No, thank you, sir. I know this meeting will be painful for both of you, and I really don't want to make it last any longer than it absolutely has to."

The old man nodded gratefully. Slowly – and obviously painfully – he lowered himself into one of the two matching armchairs. His wife, with less difficulty, sat down in the other.

"How can we help you?" the old man asked.

How *could* they help him? Rutter wondered. The instinct he had gradually developed while working under Cloggin'-it Charlie's guidance told him that at least part of the solution to Gerhard Schultz's murder lay in Germany, but he had no idea what that part might be.

He asked himself how Woodend would have handled this situation. "Why don't you tell me a little about your son," he suggested softly.

The old man bowed his head. "What can I say about him? He was a quiet, serious boy. He studied hard. He went to church regularly. He was never in any trouble."

"Did he have any girlfriends I might talk to?" Rutter asked, still groping in the dark.

Herr Schultz hesitated for several seconds, as if he could not decide how to answer the question.

"No, no girlfriends," he said finally. "As I've already told you, he was a quiet boy."

"What about his male friends, then? Are there any of them still living in the town?"

"He had one very good friend. His name was Max Ebert. He came from Karlsbruch."

Inspector Kohl did a rapid calculation. "Karlsbruch is about thirty kilometres from here, isn't it?" he said.

"Yes, it is," Herr Schultz agreed.

The inspector frowned, indicating that something in the old man's answer had puzzled him. "Thirty kilometres was a long way to travel before the war," he said. "I lived in a village myself, and I never knew anyone from so far away. How did your son come to meet this Max?"

As with the question on girlfriends, this seemed to disconcert the old man, and once again he didn't seem to know how to reply.

"Gerhard had a cousin – Johann – who came from Karlsbruch," he said falteringly. "It was while he was visiting Johann that Gerhard met Max. At that time, Johann and Max were the best of friends, though later they were to quarrel and ... but that's not important."

Wasn't it? Rutter wondered. Then why did the old man seem so reluctant to talk about it?

He contemplated pushing Schultz further

on the point, and would have done if he hadn't heard Woodend's voice in his head, telling him that the time to push was later, when he'd found out the things the old man was willing to tell him.

"Does this Max Ebert still live in Karlsbruch?" the sergeant asked Herr Schultz.

"I don't know. I don't even know if he returned home in 1945. Many of those who were sent away didn't."

There was still a reluctance there, Rutter thought. It was almost as if every question he asked skirted around the edges of a guilty secret which the old man was trying desperately to protect.

Try a fresh tack an' see where that leads you, lad, Woodend's voice said in his head.

"When did your son join the Luftwaffe?" Rutter asked.

"It was in 1938. He could see that a war was coming – we all could." The old man looked down at his gnarled hands. "As a loyal German he felt it was his duty to play his part, but it had to be the right part. He did not want to follow the path his cousin Johann had chosen."

Johann, again, Rutter noted. He thought he was beginning to understand what was going on. The old man *was* trying to hide a guilty secret, he was sure of that now. But at

249

the same time he had an urge to confess it –
to seek absolution by an open declaration.
And so he had reached a compromise with
himself – he would drop the clues, and it
was up to the English policeman either to
ignore them or to gather them up.

"Do you have any recent letters from your
son I might have a look at?" he asked.

The old man shook his head. "While he
was in the prisoner-of-war camp, he wrote
as often as he was allowed. There were a few
letters which came after the war, too. Then
they stopped. We have not heard from our
youngest son for a long, long time."

There was a great bitterness in the old
man's words, Rutter thought, but he didn't
get the impression that the bitterness was
directed towards Gerhard.

"Did he tell you in the last letter you
received why he was going to stop writing to
you?"

"No, but it is easy enough to guess the
reason. I think it was because he had a new
life in England and he wanted to put the
past behind him." The old man's voice
cracked. "I ... I also think it was because he
had grown ashamed of us – ashamed of
what we did under Hitler."

"What *did* you do under Hitler?" Rutter
asked, and even as he spoke he was dreading
the answer.

"Nothing!" the old man replied, with sudden fierceness and fire. "We did *nothing*! We tell ourselves now that we had no idea what was going behind the barbed wire of the extermination camps, but deep inside we know that we are lying. We did have an idea. More than an idea. But we were too afraid for our own skins to do anything about it."

"I don't think you should blame yourselves," Bob Rutter said sympathetically. "I've no real idea what it was like living in the Third Reich, but I'm sure that it can't have been easy—"

"Doing what is right is never easy," the old man interrupted. "But that does not mean that it should not be done. Gerhard stood up for what he believed in. And so did Max."

"Was he in the Luftwaffe, too?"

"No. Max would not fight, even for the country he loved. He did not believe in violence of any kind."

"Tell him about Max," muttered the old lady, speaking for the first time. "Tell him about what happened in the church."

"Max belonged to a small group which was helping Jews to get out of Germany," Herr Schultz explained. "But it was not an easy thing to do, and they had to wait for the right opportunity. And while they were waiting, they hid the Jews in the vault of the parish church. Somehow the SS found out what was going on. They raided the church, and took the Jews away. They took Max away, too. We heard he had been sent to a concentration camp."

"Gerhard found out what had happened when he came home on leave," Frau Schultz said, picking up the story. "He turned black with rage. We didn't want him to do it, but he drove over to Karlsbruch to confront the officer who had had Max arrested. I think he would have killed the man if he'd found him – but by that time he wasn't there any more."

"Do you happen to have a picture of your son?" Rutter asked. "And possibly a picture of his friend Max."

"Yes, we have a picture," said the old woman, rising slowly to her feet. "They are both in it."

She hobbled across to the sideboard, picked up a photograph in a silver frame, and handed it over to Rutter. There were two young men in the photograph. They were standing at what looked like the edge of a forest. The one on the left was tall and handsome, and was staring confidently at the camera. Rutter remembered the dead man he had seen in the morgue at Maltham – with the left-hand side of his face battered to a bloody pulp – and forced himself to suppress a shudder.

"That is Max," said the old woman, pointing at the other figure in the photograph.

Rutter studied him. Max was much shorter and plumper than his friend. There was none of Gerhard's confidence in his expression. He seemed, if anything, mild and unassuming. Yet behind his diffidence there must have been great strength, Rutter thought – because this man had been willing to pay the price of taking on Hitler's Reich.

"When was this taken?" he asked.

Schultz and his wife exchanged glances. "I think it was in the spring of 1936," the old man said. "It couldn't have been any later than that, because otherwise Johann—"

He'd come to an abrupt halt again, but Rutter's mind was already off on an entirely different track. There was something wrong with the photograph. The composition seemed slightly wrong, the whole view just a little skewed. Then he noticed that the left-hand edge was not quite straight, and understood why it looked wrong.

"This picture used to be bigger, didn't it?" he asked.

"Yes."

"There was a third person standing next

to Max and Gerhard, wasn't there? And you've cut him out of it?"

"Yes, again."

"Who was that third person?"

Herr Schultz sighed, as if the time for evasion was finally over – as if the English policeman had collected the clues as he'd been supposed to, and now the moment had come to bring the skeleton out of the cupboard.

"Can't you guess who he was?" he asked.

Of course he could guess! And now he knew what their secret was, too. The Schultzes had done nothing to oppose Hitler, and they were ashamed of it, but they were even more ashamed that a member of their family – their own flesh and blood – had been one of Hitler's monsters.

"The man you cut out was Gerhard's cousin, Johann," Rutter said.

"Yes."

"And the reason he and Max Ebert quarrelled was because Johann had joined the SS in summer of 1936? That's how you know the photograph couldn't have been taken later than the spring of 1936. Because Max would never have posed with Johann after that."

"Again, yes."

"And the officer who raided the church

and sent Max away to the camp – that was Johann as well?"

"That is why I cut him out of the photograph," the old woman said. "He did not belong in the same picture as two fine young men like Gerhard and Max."

"Where is Johann now?"

"Who knows?" Herr Schultz said. "By the end of the war he was a full colonel in the SS. Like many others of his kind, he went into hiding when the Allies invaded. He was tried *in absentia* by the Nuremberg Tribunal for his war crimes, and was sentenced to death. But since they couldn't find him, the sentence was never carried out."

"So no one knows what happened to him?"

The old man shrugged. "We know nothing for certain, but sometimes we hear rumours."

"What kinds of rumour?"

"That he drowned himself in the Rhine to avoid the humiliation of being executed. That he had plastic surgery on his face, and is now living quite openly in Frankfurt..."

"That he escaped to some other country," Frau Schultz said.

"Ah yes," the old man agreed. "It is possible he was spotted in Bremerhaven in November 1946. Your soldiers searched for him, but he was nowhere to be found. There are those who believed that he stowed away on a ship and escaped to United States."

Or to England! Rutter thought. Or to bloody England!

Fifteen

The clouds which had been hanging threateningly over the park all day had finally opened, and heavy rain lashed against the elegant windows of the Westbury Social Club.

Woodend stood at the bar, watching the raindrops slithering their erratic paths down the glass. Unless the weather cleared up very soon, there would be no appearances by the Dark Lady that night, he thought, because people would stay indoors – and there was little point in being a ghost if there was nobody about to see you.

The door swung open, and Simon Hailsham marched into the room. He was carrying a black umbrella. When he saw Woodend, he came to an abrupt halt, pointed the umbrella in the chief inspector's direction, and shook it vigorously. Drops of moisture fell on to the carpet, staining it, temporarily, a darker shade.

I bet he wishes it was a rifle he was pointin' at me, instead of a brolly, Woodend thought.

Hailsham furled his umbrella and hooked it on to the bar. "I suppose that you think you were very smart, Chief Inspector, getting those Poles arrested for moon-shining," he growled.

Woodend took a sip of his pint. "Aye, it wasn't a bad stroke to pull," he said complacently.

"Well, I personally don't see why them being involved in one thing necessarily rules them out from being involved in the other. Say Gerhard had found out about the still and was threatening to expose them?"

"Why would he have waited?" Woodend asked. "It would have been the simplest thing in the world to pick up the telephone an' call the local cop shop. Besides, if he'd known he was a threat to the Poles, do you really think he'd have gone wanderin' off in the woods on his own?"

"It seems unlikely," Hailsham conceded reluctantly. "But even if that wasn't the case, they still had motive enough. You can't deny the fact that they probably hated him just for being German."

"Yes, they probably did," Woodend agreed. "In fact, Zbigniew Rozpedek told me that he *should* have killed Schultz. But you don't dump shit in your own back yard."

"I beg your pardon!" Hailsham exclaimed, as if he were outraged that a policeman should use such language.

"If they'd been behind the murder, we'd have found the body miles away from their still." Woodend explained. He lit up a Capstan Full Strength. "I'm glad you came in tonight," he continued, "because I really think it's about time that you an' me had a serious talk, Mr Hailsham."

"Oh, you do, do you?" the personnel officer asked aggressively. "And if I *don't* think we should?"

Woodend grinned. "You don't have to talk to me, but I think you'd be making a serious mistake not to."

Something in Woodend's tone seemed to set off alarm bells in Hailsham's head. He stood there indecisively for a few seconds, then glanced at Tony the bar steward – who was pretending not to listen – and said, "Let's go over to one of the tables, shall we?"

He led the chief inspector to the table furthest from the bar. "What's this all about?" he asked when they'd sat down.

"I've been thinkin' back to the night Gerhard Schultz was killed," Woodend said. "You an' him were standin' at the bar, talkin'."

"I know all that."

"You talked about the situation at work, an' you talked about the appearance of the Dark Lady, but – an' this has been botherin' me for quite a time – you didn't talk about flyin'."

"Why should we have?" Hailsham asked defensively.

"I go to the Old Comrades' reunions now an' again," Woodend told him. "A lot's happened to all of us since we were demobbed. We should have plenty to tell each other about how our lives have gone, an' we all start with that – but somehow we always seem to end up yatterin' on about the war. Yet you get two fliers together for the evenin', with the drink flowin' free, an' they never even mention it. Did the pair of you *ever* discuss your wars, Mr Hailsham?"

"No, not much," Hailsham mumbled in reply. "Gerhard didn't seem to want to."

"Well, that must certainly have been a relief for you," Woodend said, "but I wonder why *he* was so reticent. I suppose real heroes are like that. You know – naturally modest. An' he was a *real* hero, wasn't he? *He* won an Iron Cross for his bravery."

"Where's all this leading?" Hailsham demanded, with an edge of panic creeping into his voice.

"I thought at first that you'd really got

somethin' against the Poles," Woodend said. "But you hadn't, had you? It's true you wouldn't have minded seein' them arrested for the murder of Gerhard Schultz, but then you wouldn't have minded anybody else bein' arrested, either – as long as it brought a swift end to the investigation."

"I don't know what you're talking about."

"Of course you do. You've been terrified for days that I'd get around to investigatin' you."

"I have nothing to hide," Hailsham said weakly.

"There *was* a Group Captain Hailsham with your squadron. I've had my sergeant check that out. He was a very brave man, by all accounts. He was shot down over the English Channel in 1940. They never found his body. An' his name wasn't Simon – it was Roger."

"Now, look here..." Hailsham protested.

"There was also a Simon Hailsham," Woodend continued. "Only he wasn't a group captain. But he did play a valuable part in the Battle of Britain – the planes would never have got off the ground if it hadn't been for corporal mechanics. Who was Roger? Your brother?"

"My cousin," Hailsham muttered, staring down at his drink.

He looked up again, and in his eyes there

was the look of an imploring puppy which has wet on the floor and is begging not to be beaten – even though it knows full well that that is exactly what's going to happen.

"What are you going to do?" he asked.

"Do?" Woodend repeated.

"Who are you going to tell? My boss?"

"I don't like you very much, Mr Hailsham," Woodend said. "I haven't from the start. But then I don't like a company which tips chemical waste into the countryside, either. All in all, I tend to think you an' BCI probably deserve one another." He lit up another Capstan Full Strength. "So I might just be persuaded to hold my tongue if..."

"If what?"

"One of the reasons the chief constable is givin' me all this grief is because he's gettin' grief himself, from BCI. They're puttin' pressure on for a quick result – an' I'd like that pressure eased a little. Do you think you could arrange it for me, Group Captain?"

"You don't know how high up this thing has gone," Hailsham said. "Our vice-chairman had lunch with someone senior from Scotland Yard yesterday. I'm only a little fish in a big pond. There may be nothing I can do."

"But you'll at least try?"

"I don't have much choice, do I?" Hailsham asked gloomily.

"No," Woodend agreed. "I don't think you do."

It was a bad line, and Rutter was forced to shout. "Can you hear me, sir?" he bawled down the receiver.

"Just about," Woodend responded faintly.

"Gerhard Schultz had a cousin called Johann. He was in the SS, and is still wanted as a war criminal. There's just a chance that he escaped to England in November 1946."

"But what's that got to do with the investigation that we're conductin'?"

"Possibly nothing. But if you remember, that Thompson chap I talked to in London told me that Gerhard Schultz had got a letter from Germany some time in November '46, and a couple of days after that he said he had to go up to Liverpool on business."

"An' are you suggestin' that the business he talked about was meetin' his cousin?"

"Again, it's a possibility."

"But what I don't see is why a man who'd just landed himself a very good job would run the risk of consortin' with a war criminal? What's your explanation for that? Family loyalty?"

"Quite the opposite," Rutter told him. "It was his cousin Johann who'd arrested

263

Gerhard's best friend, Max, and sent him off to a concentration camp. Gerhard's father is convinced that if he'd been able to find Johann back in Germany in 1939, he'd have killed him on the spot. Maybe that's what he went up to Liverpool for – to finally get his revenge."

"This isn't makin' sense," Woodend said. "If Johann knew how Gerhard felt about him – an' surely he must have done – why would he have let him know he was landin' in England?"

"Maybe he was desperate," Rutter suggested. "So desperate that he had to hope he could talk Gerhard into helping him. Or maybe the letter Gerhard received wasn't from Johann at all. It could have been from Max, or someone else who had good reason to hate Johann – and since he was in the SS, I should think there'd be any number of them."

There was a pause, then Woodend said, "Liverpool's only a short run from here. I'll slip over there in the mornin' an' see if the local bobbies know about anythin' unusual that happened in November 1946. An' what will you be doin' at the taxpayers' expense in sunny Germany?"

"I'm going to go to Karlsbruch and see if I can find Gerhard's friend Max," Rutter said.

It had stopped raining just after five o'clock, and the sun had put in a brief appearance to evaporate the moisture. Dry ground and a dark night – the perfect conditions for a ghost on horseback.

Using his torch to pick his way carefully over the slippery stones of the canal tow-path, Woodend headed towards the bridge. It was around eleven o'clock, he estimated, which should mean that he would be in just the right place at just the right time.

He reached the foot of the bridge, and climbed the dogleg path up to the road. If his suspicions were correct, he thought as he took a turn to the left, then what he was looking for wouldn't be very far away.

He found it less than fifty yards from the bridge, parked on a dirt track which ran off the lane towards a nearby farm. Other vehicles which passed by – and there would be few enough of them at that time of night – wouldn't even notice it unless they were specifically expecting to see it. And why should anybody expect to see a Land-rover and horsebox on this road?

From the other side of the horsebox, someone coughed.

Woodend raised his torch. "This is the police," he said. "You'd better come out, Mr Bernadelli."

Slowly and reluctantly, the man stepped from behind the box. Woodend angled the torch so it was playing on the man's bushy moustache.

"You weren't at home, as you claimed, the night Gerhard Schultz was killed, were you?" the chief inspector asked. "You were right here, waitin' for your Dark Lady."

"Yes," Bernadelli admitted.

"Well, now we've established that fact, you can bugger off."

"But I am responsible for the box," the Italian protested. "It is the property of Miss Maitland's riding school."

"I know it bloody is. An' has Polly Maitland herself given you permission to use it?"

"I have my own set of keys," Bernadelli said – which was as good as admitting that he hadn't got permission at all.

"Don't worry about the box," Woodend told him. "I'll look after it for now. If you want to finish the job you've been paid for, come back in half an hour – when me an' the ghost have had our little talk."

Bernadelli squared his shoulders with injured dignity. "I was not *paid* to do anything," he said, then he turned his back on the chief inspector and started to walk slowly away.

Woodend uncorked his hip flask, took a sip of whisky, and listened intently. For the first couple of minutes there was only the sound of the insects, but then he began to discern a soft, rhythmical plopping sound.

She was coming! The Dark Lady was coming!

He positioned himself deep in the shadows, and waited. The plopping sound got louder and louder. Then it stopped, but now he could hear the snorting of the horse.

"Luigi?" said a woman's voice. "Where are you, Luigi?"

Woodend switched on his torch and shone it on the animal's legs. As he'd suspected, the area around the hooves had been swathed in rags. He raised the torch higher so it was shining on the face of the startled rider.

"Good evenin', Miss Driver," he said. "I warned you your job was reportin' the news, not makin' it, didn't I?"

The journalist dismounted, took off her long wig, and threw it to the ground in disgust.

"How did you know?" she asked.

"Know what? That the Dark Lady wasn't actually a ghost? I don't believe in ghosts, lass. Besides, phantom ladies ride on phantom horses, an' phantom horses don't generally leave fresh dung on the road – an' that's what I slipped in when I was chasin' after you the other night."

"I don't mean that. I mean, how did you know it was me?"

"Oh, that was easy," Woodend told her. "Knowin' how involved he was with horses, I thought right from the start that Luigi Bernadelli would be in on the act. An' when I was up at the ridin' school, askin' Miss Maitland questions about him, I took the opportunity to have a look at the ledger. You've been takin' ridin' lessons, haven't you, Miss Driver?"

"I should have taken them somewhere further away," Elizabeth Driver said. "Chester, or Stoke."

"Aye, that would have been wise," Woodend agreed. "What were you hopin' to get out of it when you started this caper?"

"Not a lot at first. A modest article on one of the inside pages of a national daily. Novelty value. And then, the night after I'd made my first appearance, someone was actually killed. It was a tremendous stroke of luck and I could see the potential for a front page splash."

"An' why did you carry on doin' it?"

"To keep the story alive. Without the Dark Lady, this is a boring little murder."

"Bernadelli claims you weren't payin' him anythin' for helpin' you," Woodend said, changing the subject.

"He's telling the truth. I wasn't."

"So why did he agree do it?"

"Because he's a kind man who wants to see a struggling journalist get on?" Elizabeth Driver suggested hopefully.

"Or because you've been sleepin' with him."

"I did no such thing!"

"But you certainly held out the possibility that you might well in the future, didn't you?"

"I may have said some things which perhaps he interpreted in the wrong way," Miss Driver conceded.

Woodend could picture it. Elizabeth Driver, with her plan to appear as the Dark Lady already fully formed in her mind, taking her riding lessons but still not quite sure how she could get hold of a horse and box. Luigi Bernadelli, helping her on to the horse, letting his hand slip on to her buttocks whenever he thought Polly Maitland wasn't looking. Elizabeth Driver had recognised Bernadelli for the kind of man he was – a feller with his brains located squarely in his pants – and had made him an offer which proved irresistible to him. No wonder there had been so much giggling and innuendo on the Italian table when Woodend had asked where Bernadelli was the night before – he might not have slept with Elizabeth, but he had certainly told his friends that he had.

Elizabeth Driver sighed. "So what happens now?"

"I don't rightly know," Woodend admitted. "Strictly speakin', you haven't committed a crime. There's no law I'm aware of that says you can't ride along a country lane late at night wearin' a long wig, if that's what you feel like. You haven't even told any lies. I've been readin' your pieces in the papers very carefully an' you never make any claims yourself – you only quote what other people think."

"Yes, that really was rather clever of me, wasn't it?" Elizabeth Driver said. "Sort of makes up for the mistake I made over the having the riding lessons too close to home."

"Yes, it was very clever," Woodend agreed. "So, as you've probably already worked out for yourself, I can't touch you."

"I *had* worked it out actually," the reporter said complacently.

"This whole Dark Lady pantomime's got to stop, you know" Woodend told her.

"It will stop. Tonight was going to be my last night anyway. The story's just about been worked to death."

"An' you do realise that I'm goin' to have to let all the newspapers know you've been connin' them."

Elizabeth Driver gasped with surprise. "But why should you want to do that?" she asked.

"There's two reasons," Woodend said. "The first is that they've got a right to know they paid out good money for a pack of lies. The second is that if I let you get away with it this time, God only knows what stunt you'll come up with when next you feel the need for national coverage."

"Please don't tell!" Elizabeth Driver said, in a little-girl voice. "I promise I'll never do it again."

"You might say that, but you don't even believe that now," Woodend replied. "How will you feel about it next week? It won't seem like a promise at all by then. So you see how I'm fixed – I have to tell them."

The journalist moved closer to him – almost uncomfortably close, it seemed to him.

"I can be very appreciative when people do nice things for me," she said, her voice now silky and seductive, "and unlike Luigi Bernadelli, you wouldn't have to wait to get your reward."

Woodend took a step back. "I'm not quite as big a fool as that Italian feller," he said, "but even if I was, my tastes would run to somebody a bit older than you."

The journalist flicked her head back

defiantly. "All right, go ahead and tell the nationals," she said haughtily. "But before you do, *I'll* tell *you* what the result will be. Some of the papers will be shocked that I've tricked them into printing a false story. But there's a couple of them – and we both know which ones I'm talking about – that will offer me a job on the spot, because making up stories is just what they do best."

"You're probably right, lass," Woodend agreed, "but even if I do fail to throw a spanner in the works of your already dubious career, I've at least got to give it a shot, haven't I?"

Sixteen

It was a fine morning when Woodend set out from Westbury Park for Liverpool police headquarters, but the skies began to darken as the police Wolsey travelled along the East Lancs Road, and by the time the car entered the city, drizzle was pounding against the windscreen.

The Wolsey pulled up in front of the police station. Woodend got out and, ignoring the rain, stopped briefly to breathe in the same air as had once been breathed in by Charles Dickens.

Strange to be able to do that, he thought. But then, time was a funny thing. It had only been a few months since he'd last been in Liverpool. On that occasion it had been to investigate the death of a young guitarist. And now here he was again, dealing with a case which could well have had its origins in a period before that young lad was even born.

Once inside the station, Woodend was taken straight to the office of Chief Inspector Albert Armstrong. The Liverpool policeman was in his early fifties, Woodend guessed. He had silvery hair and the tired, worldly eyes of a man who'd sometimes seen more than he'd have cared to.

"This particular case you're asking about happened in late November 1946," Armstrong said, when they shaken hands and sat down. "It had been a real bugger of a month. At nights, the cold cut through to the bone, but coal was still rationed, so we didn't even have the consolation of a big blazing fire to sit in front of. Most of the days were foggy – that sort of fog which seems to get under your clothes and cling to your skin. Trams were running late, deliveries weren't being made, the docks were working at half speed – you get the picture."

"I get the picture," Woodend agreed.

"The body turned up on the morning of the twentieth of November. It was lying in a shelter near the docks. Male, round about six feet tall, late twenties, stabbed with a clean thrust to the heart."

"You haven't needed to look at your notes once," Woodend said.

"I beg your pardon?"

"You've got your notes on your desk in

front of you, an' you haven't so much as glanced at them."

Armstrong grinned ruefully. "Have you ever had a case which has become an obsession with you?" he asked.

Woodend nodded. "Oh aye. More than once."

"Well, this case became my particular obsession. Not because I'd become involved with the family, as you can get during an investigation. Nor because I felt particularly sorry for the victim. I knew nothing about him, so I had no feelings one way or the other. No, what really got on my goat was that it was a case I'm sure we could have solved if we'd just made the effort."

"So why didn't you?"

"Because my boss didn't want us to make an effort. He'd just lost his son in the war, you see, and as far as he was concerned, the only good German was a dead German."

"But you weren't content to let the matter drop?" Woodend guessed. "You did some investigatin' on your own."

Armstrong nodded. "Given where he was found, there was a good chance he'd come off a ship. I checked with the port authority, and found that a cargo boat from Bremerhaven had docked the night before. There'd been no passengers, and all the crew were accounted for. If the murdered man had travelled on that boat, he'd done it as a stowaway."

"An' how easy would that have been?"

"From my own experience with stowaways, I'd have to say it wouldn't have been easy at all. But it would have been far from impossible, especially if he had the help of one of the crew."

"I see."

"Anyway, the next step should have been to contact Germany, but DCI Phillips wasn't having any of that, and as a young bobbie who'd just been made up to sergeant, I knew it would have been professional suicide to go against his wishes. So that's where the trail ended."

"What happened to what little evidence you managed to collect?" Woodend asked.

"Should have been thrown out years ago, shouldn't it? Well, I wasn't having that, because I always hoped that one day I'd get a second chance to crack the case. Is that what you've brought me, Mr Woodend? A second chance to crack the case?"

"Maybe," Woodend said cautiously. "This evidence you've got – where do you keep it?"

"I've got it in a locker down in the basement."

"Then we'd better down there an' take a look at it, hadn't we?" Woodend suggested.

"To save time, I have already rung the Karlsbruch police," Inspector Kohl said, as he drove the Mercedes out of the small town where Gerhard Schultz had grown up.

"And what were they able to tell you?" Rutter asked.

"That they are sorry, but they know nothing of the present location of Max Ebert."

Despite a slight feeling of disappointment, Rutter grinned. "So you're not so infallible, after all," he said.

Kohl hesitated between a frown and a grin, and finally settled on the grin. "Sometimes even German records are not always as comprehensive as they should be," he admitted. "However, they were able to give me one useful lead. It seems that the parish priest was there in the church the day Ebert was arrested, so perhaps he will be able to help us. And fortunately, again according to the local police, he speaks very good English, so you can interview him yourself."

It took less than half an hour to reach Karlsbruch. The village was as neat and orderly as the small town they'd just left behind, and Rutter found himself wondering how it was that the Germans seemed to have managed to eradicate any evidence of the war, while back home traces of it were all around.

The inspector pulled up in front of the church. "We could go to the priest's house," he explained, "but Mass has only just finished, so it is very likely we will find him here."

They entered the church, and the priest, who had been standing by the altar, came down the aisle to greet them. But this was not the man they were looking for, Rutter thought. He was perhaps in his middle thirties – far too young to have been in holy orders in 1939.

The priest smiled. It was a kindly benevolent smile, a smile which clearly said that he was at peace with both the world and his God. Then he spoke a few words in German.

"The Father is welcoming us to his little church," Inspector Kohl explained to Rutter. He turned back to the priest. "I am a police inspector, " he said, still speaking in English, "and this is my colleague Sergeant Bob Rutter, who is visiting us from England."

"Oh yes?" the priest said politely, the benevolent smile still in place, but now looking slightly mystified.

"We are looking for another priest," Kohl said. "The one who was here in 1939."

"That would be my predecessor, Father Joseph. But I am afraid that you have come a little late to talk to him. He has been dead for over four years now."

Inspector Kohl frowned. First the Karlsbruch police had been unable to locate the man he and Rutter were looking for, now they had given him incorrect information about the priest. This did not look at all good in front of his English visitor.

"The priest I am seeking is the one who was here the day the SS took away a man called Max Ebert," he said.

The effect on the young priest was instantaneous. The benevolent smile melted away, and was replaced by the most haunted look that Rutter thought he had ever seen in his life.

"Oh, Max," the priest groaned. "Poor, poor Max."

"You knew him?"

The priest nodded. "You have been misinformed," he said. "It was not the then parish priest, Father Joseph, who was here when they took Max Ebert away. It was me."

"You? But..."

"I was only a boy, but I was here."

"Could you tell us about it?" Rutter asked softly.

"We were hiding the Jews in the crypt,"

the priest said. "There were a dozen of them – women and children mostly, but also a couple of men. That day, when the SS came, there were only the two of us in the church, Max and myself. When we heard their vehicles pull up outside, we knew that we had been betrayed, though we didn't know by whom. I still don't know, even after all these years, who would do such a terrible thing." He stopped to wipe the sweat from his brow. "I'm sorry. This is very difficult for me."

"Take your time," Rutter said soothingly.

"They stormed into the church. There were about twenty of them. Max tried to stop them, to reason with them – but they knocked him to the ground, and began kicking him. I was a mere child. I wanted to help Max but there ... there was nothing I could do."

"Of course there wasn't," Rutter said soothingly. "Tell me what happened next."

"Half of them went down to the crypt to round up the Jews, the rest stayed behind to guard us. As if it needed ten armed men to guard a boy like me and a man who was lying on the stone floor, fighting for air! They herded the Jews up the stairs as if they were nothing more than cattle." The priest swallowed hard. "And all the time, the SS men were tormenting the prisoners. Their leader, a lieutenant called Johann Schultz, was the worst one of the lot. You would not believe the language that he used. You could never imagine the filthy, dirty way he was describing what was going to happen to them. He had an expression of sadistic ecstasy on his face. To look at him was to gaze into the very jaws of hell. And those poor people, those helpless women and little children. They looked like exactly what they were – the walking dead. I ... I..."

The priest was on the verge of either fainting or being sick, Rutter thought. "As we were driving up, did you happen to notice if there's a bar near here?" he asked Inspector Kohl.

"No I didn't," Kohl confessed. "But this is Germany – there is always a bar somewhere fairly close."

"Let me buy you a coffee, Father," Rutter said to the priest. "Or something stronger, if you feel you need it."

"Yes," the other man said. "Yes, I think that something stronger would be a good idea."

The basement of the Liverpool police station was both dank and dusty. The only illumination in the place was provided by a single naked bulb suspended from the ceiling.

"We don't use this area much any more," Chief Inspector Armstrong said apologetically.

He went to a long metal table which dominated the centre of the room, and cleaned it off with a rag he'd brought with him. "No point in contaminating the evidence at this stage of the proceedings, is there?" Once the table was cleaned to his satisfaction, he walked over to a battered grey metal locker in the far corner of the room. "Here it is. Everything I have on our mystery man."

He opened the locker and took out a suit, smelling strongly of mothballs, which he placed on the table. This was followed by shoes, a shirt, socks, underwear, an overcoat, and a short, evil-looking knife.

"No other belongings?" Woodend asked.

Armstrong shook his head. "No. As I see it, there are three possible explanations for that. The first is that he didn't have any. The second is that he hid them somewhere, shortly before the attack, and we never found them. Well, we weren't really looking, if I'm honest – not with Harry Phillips in charge of the case. And the third possibility is that the killer took them with him – perhaps they were even the motive for the attack."

There was the sound of footsteps on the

stairs, then a young constable appeared.

"Got the Chief Super on the phone, sir," he said to Armstrong. "He wants to speak to you right away."

"Bugger it!" Armstrong said. He turned back to Woodend. "Will you excuse me for a few minutes?"

"Aye, I'll be as happy as a sandboy playin' around with this lot," Woodend told him.

Armstrong disappeared up the stairs, and Woodend picked up the knife. It had been made in Sheffield, a place noted for its skill in producing precision cutting instruments. He gingerly ran his index finger over the edge of the blade. It was finely honed and razor sharp. In a competent pair of hands it could do a lot of damage, he thought.

He laid the knife back where he had found it, and picked up the overcoat. It was long and heavy – almost a trench coat. There was a narrow slash in it at just about heart level. He picked up the knife again, and slid it carefully into the gash. A perfect fit.

He turned his attention to the jacket. It was not new, but it was good quality, he decided. Probably pre-war. The label inside said it had been made by a tailor in Munich. Just below the breast pocket was the cut the knife had made as it entered the wearer's body.

He examined the shoes next. They were

very shoddy articles, the product of a country short on resources but big on demand, just as West Germany had been immediately after the war. The socks and underpants were of similar quality. The vest and shirt were a little better made. They too had a knife slash at heart level; but unlike the jacket and the overcoat, a rough circle of dirty brown stain surrounded these lacerations.

Replacing the evidence on the table, Woodend stepped back and lit up a Capstan Full Strength. The clothes had told him absolutely nothing, but there was a nagging feeling at the back of his mind that they should have done.

He let the smoke snake its way soothingly around his lungs. There was something which wasn't quite right, he told himself. One piece of clothing, or possibly two, which didn't exactly fit in with the rest.

The jacket? That was certainly of better quality than all the other stuff, but he'd already satisfactorily explained that to himself.

The shoes? No.

And suddenly, he had it! The jokers in the pack were the shirt and the vest. And what made them different was that they had no labels in them.

He picked up the shirt again. There had

been a label inside the collar – he could still find the jagged traces of the two edges – but it had been cut out. The same was true of the vest.

He reached for the knife, and slid it into the slash in the shirt. The cut was wider than the knife. Much, much wider. He repeated the experiment with the vest, and got the same result.

There was the sound of footsteps on the stairs. Woodend replaced the knife on table, and lit up a fresh Capstan Full Strength from the stub of the one he'd just been smoking.

"Bloody chief supers!" Chief Inspector Armstrong complained, as he reached the foot of the stairs. "They are the bloody limit, aren't they? Every time they've got some piffling little query they want answering, they expect you to jump like a bloody trained flea." He looked down at the evidence on the table. "Did you find anything useful?"

"No," Woodend lied. "At least, nothin' that I didn't know already. The dead man was almost certainly a feller from Bavaria, by the name of Johann Schultz. He was an officer in the SS, an' by all accounts a pretty nasty piece of work, judgin' even by their low standards."

"So who killed him?" Armstrong asked.

"That we'll never know," Woodend told him. "But does it really matter? Couldn't it be that your old boss was correct, an' that in Schultz's case at least, the only good German *was* a dead one?"

"You're probably right," Armstrong agreed. He looked down at the pile of clothes again. "After what you've told me, I suppose I might as well throw this lot out."

"Aye, you might as well at that," Woodend said.

Armstrong shook his head slowly from one side to the other. "It's a funny thing," he said, "but I've had them with me for so long that they've almost become like old friends."

The café was just opposite the Catholic church. When the waitress came over to the table, Kohl ordered steins of beer for himself and his English colleague, and a coffee and Ansbach brandy for the priest.

"I am sorry for my moment of weakness back there in the church," the priest said shakily, when he'd had a generous sip of the brandy. "How far had I got with my story?"

"You were telling us that the SS took the Jews out of the church," Rutter prompted.

"That's right. They loaded them on to an open truck and drove them away. Most of the SS men left as well, but there were still five or six of them in the church. One of them was Lieutenant Schultz. He was striding up and down with a pistol in his hand, and it was obvious, even to a child like I was at the time, that he was very drunk. As he walked, he kept shouting abuse at Max, who was being held by two of the other soldiers."

"What sorts of things was he saying?"

"At one point, he said, 'We used to be good friends, but you turned your back on me when I joined the SS, didn't you? I was hurt for a while. But not any more. Not now you've turned out to be nothing more than a Jew-lover. Who'd *want* to be friends with you now, Fat Boy?'" The priest paused for a second, as he relived the moment in his mind. "Lieutenant Schultz was lying when he said he didn't want Max to be his friend, you know," he continued. "Max had this quality about him which made everybody want him to like them."

"What else did Lieutenant Schultz say?"

"He said, 'You despise me, don't you, Fat Boy?'" The priest took another sip of his brandy. "Max wouldn't answer him, which seemed to infuriate Schultz even more. He staggered over to Max, and thrust his gun barrel right under his chin. 'What right do you have to feel superior to me?' he screamed. 'Is it your religion? Is that what it is?' And still Max was silent."

"That must have taken a lot of courage with a gun jammed against his jaw," Rutter said.

"Max had enough courage to fill the whole church, and Schultz was starting to realise it. I think he was beginning to feel very small and humiliated indeed. 'Don't you know your religion is nothing but a lot of shit?' he asked. 'Haven't you learned yet that there isn't any such thing as a god? If God existed, do you think he'd allow me to do this?' And then he turned round and pointed his gun at the statue of the Virgin in the alcove."

"How did Max react?"

"When he realised what the Lieutenant was about to do, he started to struggle, but the two SS men had a tight grip on him. Schultz took careful aim, and fired three times. Even though he was drunk, he still managed to put all three bullets into Our Lady's face. 'There you are,' he said. 'You've seen what I've done, and I'm still alive, aren't I? No thunderbolt has struck me down. There's no booming voice from heaven, telling me I've done wrong. And that's because this god of yours – which makes you think you're so much better than me – doesn't exist!'"

"What did Max say to that?"

"He spoke very quietly, but very steadily. He said, 'You must believe what you want to believe. Only time will tell which of us is right.'" The priest shook his head sadly. "I have always believed that if Max had agreed with him – had said, yes, what he'd done to the Virgin did prove that there was no God – Lieutenant Schultz would have let him go."

"Because they used to be friends?"

"No, because he would have proved that he was the superior of the two. But Max would never say anything like that, even though his life depended on it." The priest sighed. "I pray that if ever I found myself in Max's situation, I would find the strength that he did, but I can never be sure that I would."

"What happened to Max?" Rutter asked.

"Schultz gave up trying to humiliate him – he was only making himself look smaller with every attempt – and he ordered the SS to take Max away. I was spared because I was only a child, and therefore thought not to understand enough of what was going on to be really involved." The priest laughed bitterly. "If I'd been a Jewish boy they would have had no hesititation in deciding I was as guilty as Max was, but because I was pure Aryan they were prepared to believe that I'd merely been led astray by older people."

"Do you know where they took Max?"

"No one knew for sure what happened to the people who disappeared, but I heard that they took him to one of the camps. When the war was finally over, I kept hoping that he would return home, but I knew in my heart that he never would. He was arrested in 1939, you have to remember. No one could have survived the camps for six long years."

There seemed no more to say. Inspector Kohl paid the bill, and the three of them left the bar.

"Thank for all your help," Rutter said, once they were out on the street. "I can appreciate how painful it must have been for you to talk about it."

"It had to be said," the priest told him. "Would you like to come and see our Virgin before you leave?"

"Your Virgin?"

"The one Lieutenant Schultz shot at."

"You still have her?" Rutter asked, surprised.

For the first time since they had mentioned Max Ebert to him, the priest smiled.

"Yes, we still have her. She bears the scars of Nazism, but then so do the rest of us. It has always been her role to share in the suffering of all mankind. And even apart from that, she has always been a rather special Virgin. I could show you. It wouldn't take a minute."

Rutter, who had no time for religion, was on the point of declining when the feeling of shame swept through him. The Virgin was obviously important to the priest in a way he himself could probably never even begin to comprehend. It would be churlish and ungrateful, after what the man had put himself through for their benefit, not to do this one small thing for him.

"I'd consider it a great honour to see your Virgin, Father," he said.

The priest led them back into the church, and to the alcove where the Virgin stood. Rutter could see the three holes where the bullets from Johann Schultz's Luger had burrowed their way into her wooden face. He had been quite prepared for that. But what he had not been prepared for, he thought as he gasped with surprise, was the fact that what remained of the face, and the hands which were clasped together in prayer, were painted black.

"There are only a few like her in the whole of Europe," the priest said. "The most famous ones are in Krakow, Poland, and Guadeloupe in Spain, though naturally, we in this village daily commit the sin of pride by preferring our own. In English, I think you call them 'Black Madonnas'. In German, they are known as *Schwarze Jungfrau*. But we have a special name for ours, because she has seen so much suffering in her time. We call her the *Schwarze Dame*."

"And what does that mean?" Rutter asked.

"It means, 'The Black Lady'." The priest shook his head. "No, it is not quite that. The translation is too literal." He turned to Inspector Kohl for help. "Could you think of any other word I could use instead of black?"

The German policeman shrugged. "Perhaps 'dark'," he suggested. "The *Dark* Lady."

Seventeen

Woodend had left the rain behind him on the edge of Liverpool, and in Westbury Park it had turned into a truly glorious day. The chief inspector strolled leisurely through the park, past the neat houses which were really no more than disguised army barracks, and towards the woods in which he had been attacked, a German called Schultz had met a violent death and a group of Polish refugees had brewed the vodka of their homeland.

He savoured the walk, knowing that it would be the last one he ever took in this place. He felt the same uneasy mixture of emotions which always assailed him when a case was nearly over – satisfaction at having done his job well; sadness for the people whose lives had accidentally become entangled in the most primitive of human barbarities; a reluctance to leave a world which, for a few days at least, had become his world.

He reached the edge of the woods and stopped to light up a Capstan Full Strength. Had the German been taken completely by surprise by the man he met on the path to the lake that fatal night? Somehow Woodend didn't think he had. Schultz, he was beginning to suspect, hadn't been half as drunk as he'd pretended to be in the club.

He thought of Charles Dickens' *A Tale of Two Cities* – of Sidney Carton, who so resembles Charles Darney that he was able to take the other man's place on the guillotine. There were similarities to the great man's book in this investigation, though here it was more a case of "A Tale of Two Villages" – one of them in rural Cheshire, the other in distant Bavaria.

He had smoked the Capstan Full Strength so far down that he could feel the heat of the burning ash on his fingers. He dropped the cigarette, and ground it with the heel of his shoe. This was it, then, he thought. He had his solution, and there was no point in putting off what he had to do any longer. Which meant that it was time to go and see Karl Müller.

Woodend looked from the pale intense face of Karl Müller to the large iron crucifix on the wall, and back again.

"I had a phone call from my lad Sergeant

Rutter an hour ago," he told the German.

Müller shrugged. "Why should that be of any possible interest to me?" he asked

"Because he was callin' from Germany. From a small town in Bavaria. A town that goes by the name of Karlsbruch."

The German nodded, almost fatalistically. "I see."

"Yes, I think you do," Woodend agreed. "Why did you change your name when you left Germany?"

"I brought my wife and my God with me to England," Müller said. "I wanted to leave the rest of my old life behind. Does that make any sense to you, Chief Inspector?"

"Yes. After everythin' you must have been through durin' the war, I suppose it does," Woodend admitted.

He took his Capstan Full Strength out of his pocket and offered one to Müller. He noticed that, even now, at the moment of truth, the German's hand was as steady as a rock when he took the cigarette.

"When I asked you and your wife if you'd killed Gerhard Schultz, you both swore that you hadn't," the chief inspector continued.

"And I am still willing to swear to that."

"Oh, I'm sure you are," Woodend said. "After what I've learned this mornin' I'd be prepared to swear to it myself. But you do know Gerhard really is dead, don't you?"

"As much as I am unwilling to believe it, I have to admit that it seems likely," Müller said.

"Let me tell you as much of the story of how he died as I've managed to piece together," Woodend said. "At the time Gerhard Schultz was released from the prisoner-of-war camp on the south coast of England, his cousin, Johann Schultz, the SS colonel, was already on the run from the War Crimes Commission. An' he stayed on the run for well over a year. But in the end, he must have decided that his luck couldn't last for ever, and that the safest thing for him to do would be to get out of Germany altogether."

"I know none of this," Müller said.

"I know you don't. That's why I'm tellin' you. Johann stowed away on a boat to Liverpool. Gerhard found out about it. I'm not sure how – presumably he got a letter from a friend tellin' him what was happenin'. But that really doesn't matter. The thing is that when Johann arrived, Gerhard was waitin' at the docks for him. Gerhard's plan, I'm almost certain, was to kill Johann for what he'd done to his best friend Max, back in 1939. Anyway, as things turned out, it was the other way around. Johann killed Gerhard. Now we come to the important bit. Johann's standin' there over Gerhard's body, an' he has a brilliant idea. Instead of takin' on a false identity, he'll take on a real one – Gerhard's. An' in order to leave a confused trail behind him, he'll make sure the dead body the police find looks as if it belongs to a German who's just got off one of the boats. So he dresses Gerhard's body in his German jacket, trousers, shoes an' socks, an' takes his cousin's clothes for himself. Only he can't exchange shirts an' vest, because Gerhard's are already cut an' stained with his blood. Are you followin' all this?"

"Yes, I'm following it," Müller said.

"He takes the labels out of Gerhard's shirt an' vest, because he doesn't want the police askin' why somebody who's just arrived from abroad is wearin' clothes made by an English company. I was puzzled by the lack of labels even before I noticed they'd been ripped out – after all, the rest of the clothes were labelled – but I'd probably never have got to the truth if it hadn't been for the knife."

"The knife?" Müller repeated.

"Aye. There were two knives involved in the fight. One was Gerhard's, which had been made in Sheffield, an' the other was Johann's, which probably came from the Ruhr. Now the one Johann had to leave behind was Gerhard's. Can you see why, Mr Müller?"

The other man nodded his head. "He wanted the police to think a German had been attacked by an Englishman, so the knife he left had to be the English one?"

"Exactly," Woodend agreed. "So what he does is, he uses Gerhard's knife to make the slashes in his own coat an' jacket. An' a pretty good job he made of it, too. They're in just the right place to match the slashes in the shirt an' vest. But then he has a problem. You see, if his knife had had a narrower blade than Gerhard's, he could have made the cuts in the shirt an' vest bigger. But it didn't. His knife was wider, an' there was no way he could make the rips any smaller, now was there? So all he could hope for was that nobody would think to match up the knife an' the slashes. An' nobody had – until I did it this mornin'."

"I see," Müller said.

"Johann goes through Gerhard's wallet, and finds a letter which tells him not only Gerhard's address, but also that he's got a new job. Of course, there's one little detail he has to clear up before he can present himself at BCI as Gerhard, but that's soon taken care of. Now all he has to do is pick up Gerhard's belongin's, which he does in the middle of the night, so no one will see him. Friends might be upset he never said goodbye, but these things happen. The landlord might be surprised he's moved out before he had to, but he's left a month's rent, so who's goin' to complain? He takes the new job, and does very well at it, so, as from November 1946, Johann Schultz completely disappears from the face of the earth. And then he comes here. Would you like to carry on from there, sir?"

Karl Müller nodded. "When I heard that the new manager was called Mr Schultz, I never dreamed it would be someone I knew."

"Why not?"

Müller shrugged. "Why should I have? Schultz is a common enough name in Germany."

"Did you recognise him immediately?"

"Oh yes. I will never forget the face that I saw in our church on that terrible morning in 1939."

"But he didn't recognise you as Max?"

Müller shook his head. "I had changed a great deal. Six years in a concentration camp will do that to a man. Before the war I used to be overweight, but I was almost a skeleton when I was released, and since then I haven't been able to put on more than a few pounds however much I eat."

"Did you confront Schultz with his past right away?"

"No."

"So what did you do?"

A thin smile came to the German's face. "What do you think I would have done, Mr Woodend?"

It didn't take much to work it out. "I think you would have gone to church and prayed to your God for guidance," the chief inspector said.

"That's exactly what I did do."

"And did you get any?"

"Yes. The Lord told me that if Johann truly repented his sins, I was to forgive him."

Woodend recalled the piece of paper which had fallen out of the copy of *A Tale of Two Cities* which had once belonged to Schultz.

"That's why you sent him that anonymous note about the Dark Lady, isn't it?" he asked.

"I sent him several notes to remind him of his terrible crimes. It did no good. He hadn't changed."

"How can you be so sure of that?" Woodend asked, though remembering the atmosphere of evil he had sensed in Schultz's room back at Westbury Hall, he was already more than half convinced that Müller was right.

"I am sure because I went to my church every time the priest was taking confession, praying that Johann would be there, ready to unburden his conscience and cleanse his soul. He never appeared."

"Perhaps he went to another church?" Woodend pointed out, still in the role of Devil's Advocate.

"Then there was the night he died," Müller continued, dismissing Woodend's suggestion.

"What about it?"

"Schultz was drunk – not as drunk as he pretended to be, but drunk enough. He was bragging to Simon Hailsham about how he was going to save the company lots of money by getting rid of some of the labour force. And, I swear to you, it was exactly as if I were back in the church in Karlsbruch, listening to him telling the Jews what would happen to them – how they would be made to work, how the women would be forced to prostitute themselves and how, in the end, and whatever they did, they would be exterminated."

"Why did you follow him into the woods?"

"I wanted to give him one last chance to change before I denounced him to the authorities."

Woodend glanced up at the wall again. "You took your crucifix with you, didn't you?"

"When you are intending to meet a

301

demon, it is as well to have the symbol of the Lord with you."

"What happened?"

"I thought I would take him by surprise, but it was he who surprised me. He was waiting for me behind a tree. He had a knife in his hand – perhaps the same knife he killed Gerhard with. 'I knew that whoever was sending me those stupid notes would follow me,' he said. 'How do you know who I really am?' So I told him that I was Max."

"An' what did he say to that?"

"He said, 'I should have shot you back in 1939'."

"You had no doubt in your mind that he was intendin' to kill you in the woods?"

The German shook his head. "None whatsoever. But if I had had any doubts, his next words would have dispelled them."

"An' what were they?"

"He asked me if I'd told anyone else that he was *Johann* Schultz. Without thinking, I replied, 'Only my wife.' 'Then she will have to die, too,' he said. He lunged at me with his knife, but he lost his footing. Before he could regain his balance, I swung at him with my crucifix. The next thing I remember, he was lying on the ground. There was no doubt in my mind that he was dead."

"What happened to the knife?"

"I picked it up and brought it back with me. I don't know why I did that. I wasn't thinking very logically. The next day, I threw it into the lake. If you wish, I can show you where it is."

"He was the one who attacked you," Woodend said. "Why didn't you go to the police and explain the circumstances?"

"I have confessed what I did to my parish priest, and my true punishment, when it eventually comes, will be at the hands of the Lord my God," Müller said. "I have already been through six long years of living in a man-made hell and I saw no reason to allow myself to be locked up again. But now that you have discovered the truth, Mr Woodend, I will bow my head and submit to the laws of man without a struggle."

Eighteen

Bob Rutter had not thought that the first person he would see when he cleared customs and excise at London Airport would be his boss. But there Woodend was, reassuringly dressed in one of his hairy sports coats and puffing away enthusiastically at a Capstan Full Strength.

"Good flight?" the chief inspector asked his sergeant, when they'd shaken hands.

Rutter shrugged. "Pretty tolerable, I suppose."

"You weren't nervous at all?"

"Nervous?" Rutter said, with evident derision in his voice. "What on earth would I have to be nervous about? There's no more to flying than there is to taking a bus."

Woodend grinned. "I'm sure you're right, lad," he agreed. "An' maybe one day I'll even give it a try myself." His face assumed a more serious expression. "You did a good job out there on your own in Germany, Bob. No, I'm not bein' fair. It was a better-than-

304

good job. It was an excellent job. We'd never have come up with the right answers if it hadn't been for all the work you put in, an' I'm only sorry you'll not be gettin' the credit you're due."

Rutter's jaw dropped. He remembered the first case he worked on with Woodend – the murder in Salton, just a few miles away from Westbury Park – and what the chief inspector had said to the constable who'd been sent to meet them on Maltham station: *I'm a bad bugger to work for. I expect results yesterday, an' I won't stand for anybody swingin' the lead. But I'm no glory grabber. If you deserve credit, I'll see you get it.*

And that had been perfectly true, right up until that moment, but now Cloggin'-it Charlie seemed to be saying that if anyone was going to get the kudos for solving this case, it was going to be him. What had made him change so quickly? Had he suddenly decided that he had to protect his own career, whatever the cost to anybody else's?

"I've obviously got some explainin' to do, lad," the chief inspector said. "An' the best place to do it is in the bar – with a pint in my right hand."

"And a Capstan Full Strength in your left," Rutter said grimly.

"Aye," Woodend agreed, "an' with a Capstan Full Strength in my left."

305

The drinks had been bought, and Woodend was ready to begin his explanation. "There's no easy way to break this to you, Bob, so I'll come straight to the point," he said. "We're off the case."

"We're what!" Rutter gasped.

"We're off the case," Woodend repeated. "I told the commander this mornin' that I no longer have the confidence of the chief constable of Cheshire, an' it would be better if he sent another team up there. I've handed all the evidence I've collected over to the Cheshire police. Well ... some of it, anyway."

"But how could you do that!" Rutter protested. "We had the bloody thing cracked!"

"Did we?"

"Of course we did. It's obvious from what we've learned that Gerhard Schultz was really Johann Schultz—"

"So you've put the Johann an' Gerhard thing together without even seein' the clothin' evidence Chief Inspector Armstrong had saved from oblivion," Woodend said. "How d'you manage it, lad?"

"The neighbour I talked to in London hinted – as much as he dared, given the law on such things – that he and Gerhard had what you might call a 'special' relationship. When I talked to Gerhard's father, he looked very sheepish when I asked him about Gerhard's girlfriends."

"So what do you infer from that?"

"That until November 1946, Gerhard was, at the very least, a latent homosexual. But after that November, he was suddenly chasing everything in a skirt. And not just chasing them. Remember how the prostitute in Hereford told me that he used to dress up in a uniform, then hurl abuse at her in German and follow that with a whipping?"

"Yes, I remember."

"She didn't notice anything about his uniform, but I'm prepared to bet it had SS insignia on it."

"So am I," Woodend agreed.

"So when you add all that up, there's only one possible explanation. The man calling himself Gerhard before that date and the one calling himself Gerhard after it are not the same people."

"Well done, lad," Woodend said approvingly.

But Rutter was not looking for praise from his boss at that moment. "And once we know that Max is now calling himself Karl Müller," he pressed on, "and that's obvious after what I discovered in Germany, because only Max and the priest knew about the Dark Lady..."

"Agreed."

"Then I would have thought that we'd plenty of evidence for pulling Müller in."

"Johann Schultz was in the SS," Woodend said heavily, "so God only knows how much blood he had on his hands. But two deaths we do know about for sure. First there was his cousin Gerhard, an' then there was Arthur Fanshaw, the personnel manager at BCI's Hereford plant."

"You're certain Johann killed him?"

"Either that, or it was a coincidence – a bloody big coincidence. Look at the facts. Johann reads the letter Fanshaw sent to Gerhard – the letter Gerhard carries around his wallet. An' what does he learn from that? He learns that Gerhard's been offered a good job, an' the only person from BCI who's met him is Fanshaw. Then a couple of days after that, poor old Arthur's knocked down by a hit-an'-run driver. Come on, Bob, it's stretching things a bit far not to see the two things as interconnected."

"You're right," Rutter agreed.

"So on the one side you've got Johann Schultz, an' on the other you've got Max – or Karl Müller, as he's known these days. Johann behaved like a monster, an' went unpunished for over twenty years. Max tried to save some Jews from the gas chamber, an' got six years of livin' hell for his pains. He also told me that he killed Johann in self-defence – an' I believe him. So which one do you think had the right to walk away scot free?"

Bob Rutter looked down into his beer. "That's all very well, but there's the law to consider," he said.

"If it'll make it any easier for you to accept, lad, why don't you look on Max Ebert's six years in the camp as sort of payin' in advance for a crime he hadn't committed yet."

Rutter lit up one of his cork-tipped cigarettes. The anger and sense of betrayal he had felt earlier was gone, but in their place had come worry, as a hundred questions hit him at once.

"What if the new men the commander sends up to Cheshire solve the crime?" he asked. "Have you thought of that? We'll look a complete pair of idiots, won't we?"

"They won't solve it," Woodend assured him. "I've told them nothin' about what you discovered in Germany, an' I've even thrown in a couple of red herrin's to send them chargin' off up blind alleys."

"But when they discover – as they're bound to – that Gerhard Schultz was really Johann Schultz—"

"An' how will they find out that?"

Rutter sighed. It was not like his boss to be

so thick. "From the Liverpool police," he said.

"The Liverpool police don't know. I told Chief Inspector Armstrong that their stiff was Johann."

"Why?" Rutter asked, his anger returning. "Because you'd got this nice little perversion of the course of justice planned all along?"

Woodend shook his head. "At the time I said it, I hadn't spoken to you, an' I'd no idea who the killer was, so I certainly wasn't doin' anythin' to cover his tracks for him."

"So why didn't you tell Armstrong the truth?"

"Because he'd then have been obliged to tell Gerhard's parents," Woodend explained.

"So what?"

"It's bad enough them knowin' their son's dead now, without them learnin' that he's been gone for fifteen years, an' was killed by his own cousin. At least this way they'll be able to kid themselves into thinkin' that he had a few happy years before he met his end."

You never cease to amaze me, you old bugger, Rutter thought. But aloud, all he said was, "It's all very well you being so magnanimous, sir, but it'll be a black mark against my record."

"I'm the feller who was in charge of the

case," Woodend said. "If anybody's goin' to take the blame for not closin' it, it'll be me."

"Mud sticks," Rutter told him. "Once you've been associated with a failure, you're marked for life."

Woodend sighed. "I'll tell you what, lad. If you really want us to arrest Karl Müller, we can go back to Cheshire right now an' do it. An' I really mean that. You only have to say the word, an' we'll do it."

Rutter opened his mouth and tried to will himself into saying, 'OK, let's do it,' but the words just wouldn't come.

Cloggin'-it Charlie had got things right again, he thought – God damn the bloody man!

Epilogue

It was late afternoon. Woodend sat across the desk from Commander Greaves. There was a distinct chill in the atmosphere which had nothing at all to do with the room temperature.

"You really screwed things up this time, didn't you, Charlie?" the commander asked.

Woodend shrugged, wondering what special skill it took to make the use of his first name sound so much like an insult.

"So I didn't come back with a result this time," he said. "Nobody's got a perfect record – an' mine's a bloody sight better than most."

"I'm not just talking about results," the commander said, with an edge of anger slipping into his voice, which Woodend thought might merely be there for effect. "I'm talking about the fact that in a few short days you've managed to piss off one chief constable and one very large chemical

312

company. And it's not the first time some-thing like that's happened either."

"An' it probably won't be the last," Woodend replied.

"You might be wrong about that, Charlie – at least as far as the Yard's concerned."

Woodend felt his heart suddenly start to beat a little faster. What was his boss saying to him? he wondered. Or did he really wonder at all? Weren't the commander's words open to only one possible interpretation?

He thought about living a life in which he wasn't a policeman – and found the notion inconceivable. However frustrating he found his work, however much it sometimes sickened him, he was a bobby through and through.

He took a deep breath. "Would you mind explainin' that last remark, sir?" he asked.

Greaves lit up a Player's Navy Cut. Woodend watched as the grey smoke spiralled into the air, like a dangerous snake which seemed languid, but was always ready to strike.

"If you had have got a result, you'd probably have saved your skin – at least until the next time you got up the nose of someone important," the commander said. "But you didn't get a result. You've absolutely no idea who killed Gerhard

Schultz, now have you?"

Though the commander didn't know it, he had just opened a loophole. All Woodend had to do was produce the name of Karl Müller, like an ace from up his sleeve, and he was in the clear. And what would Müller get for his crime. Four years? Maybe even less than that? It was even possible, given that Johann Schultz was a war criminal, that he might not serve any time at all.

He closed his eyes and pictured the concentration camp he had seen for himself during the Allied invasion of Germany. The hollow eyes of the starving prisoners. The feeling of desperation which was so great that those prisoners could not even rejoice in their own liberation. Karl Müller had come through all that, had regained his faith in God, and had even been willing to forgive Johann Schultz if he'd shown the slightest sign of repentance.

"I said, you've no idea who killed Gerhard Schultz, have you?" the commander repeated.

"No, sir," Woodend replied, "I haven't got a clue."

"So I've had to send a fresh team up to Cheshire to sort out your mess, which means you're about as deep in the shit as it's possible to be."

"There's a move to get me dismissed, is

314

there?" Woodend asked – though he didn't know why he even bothered to state such an obvious inference.

"It's more than a move. The Top Brass are tired of having to apologise for you, tired of having to patch things up after you've been through your 'bull in a china shop' routine."

So the unthinkable really was about to happen. "I won't take it lyin' down, you know," Woodend warned the commander.

"You know Jack Dinnage, don't you, Charlie?" Greaves asked, totally out of the blue.

"Aye, he was my inspector when I first joined the force. We got on well. But what's that got to do with ... ?"

"You may not know it, but he's recently been appointed the chief constable of Central Lancashire."

"Good for him," Woodend said. "I'm very pleased. He deserves it. But I thought it was *my* future we were talkin' about."

"It is. For some reason I don't pretend to understand, Jack wants you to work for him."

Woodend saw exactly what Greaves had been doing – first paint the situation as hopeless, and then throw the drowning man a lifeline. But it wasn't a lifeline he was prepared to grasp at just yet.

"Will there be a promotion in it for me if I

agree to move?" he asked.

"Don't push your luck," the commander growled.

"I could fight you over this," Woodend said. "I could set the Police Federation on you."

"And what would be the point of that?" the commander asked, shaking his head. "Even if you won – and I don't think there's much chance of that – there'd be so much bad blood that you wouldn't ever want to work for the Yard again. And you wouldn't have the Lancashire job to fall back on, either."

The bastard was right, Woodend thought. He was dead bloody right. Anyway, why should he even want to stay in London? He was a northerner who had never quite come to terms with living in the south. And who was to say the cases which came the way of a regional police force wouldn't be every bit as interesting as the ones handled by the Yard? Of course, it would mean losing Bob Rutter, who was the best bagman he'd ever had but...

"I'll take the job on one condition," he said.

"And what's that?" the commander asked suspiciously.

"My sergeant gets a promotion."

"But he's only held his present rank for

five minutes," the commander protested.

"He's a quick learner," Woodend countered. "He's picked up more in them five minutes he's been my sergeant than a lot of bobbies do in a whole lifetime on the job."

The commander shook his head dismissively. "We can't have him leapfrogging other applicants. The Yard doesn't work like that."

"He wouldn't be in the Yard. I'd want to take him with me to the Mid-Lancs force."

Greaves stubbed his cigarette exasperatedly in the ashtray. "For God's sake, talk sense! Even if I agree, your sergeant probably wouldn't want the job if it was offered to him."

"He'd take it," Woodend assured him. "He's far too ambitious a lad to turn down a quick promotion. Besides, we're a good team, an' he won't want to see us split up."

"So you think he'll move up to the darkest north just so he can still work with you?" the commander asked incredulously. "You've got a very high opinion of yourself, haven't you?"

"Aye, an' I think a lot of young Bob Rutter an' all. So what's it goin' to be, sir? Do we have a fight on our hands – you an' me – or do you agree to give me what I want?"

"If it was left up to me, I'd tell you to go hell," the commander said, and now the anger in his voice was definitely real.

"But ... ?" Woodend asked.

Greaves sighed. "But since Jack Dinnage is so keen to have you working with him, I expect he'll go along with the deal."

It was towards dusk, and the sky was filled with crimson swirls. Woodend walked slowly along the Embankment, looking down at the river which had, for so long, been the very heart of the city. Yet it was not quite the vital heart it had once been. When he'd first come to London, just after the war, it had been chock-a-block with traffic – liners, cargo vessels, tugs – but not any more.

Things change, he thought. Sometimes they change so slowly that we hardly notice it happening – but they change all the same. How long had it been since he'd been an earnest young bobbie just starting out on his first solo beat? Half a lifetime ago! And yet it seemed to have passed in the blink of an eye.

He thought of Joan, who had been a slim girl when he married her, but now had settled into comfortable matronly plumpness. And of Annie, a tiny baby he had held in his arms who would soon be bringing her first boyfriend home for Sunday afternoon tea.

Yes, things changed, and he should never